DANCE ON THE MOON

J. L. WELLS

Copyright © 2013 J. L. Wells
All rights reserved

No part of this publication may be reproduced, distributed, or transmitted in any form or by any means, including photocopying, recording, or other electronic or mechanical methods, without prior written permission of the publisher, except in the case of brief quotations embodied in critical reviews and certain non commercial uses permitted by copyright law.

First published by sistarsofthemoon publishing
2013
London UK

Cover design from an original oil painting by Jaqui Wells

Also by this author:

Midsummer Solstice

To catch a cry

Acknowledgements

Thanks to my wonderful sister Kay for painstakingly typing out the first drafts of my hand written manuscripts. In the very beginning of my venture helping this book to eventually come into fruition. Also thanks to Ben Bryant for all his help and patience in the correct formatting of my book.

They say there is magic buried deep in this earth waiting to be discovered. We are part of the earth. Magic is in our very being. There are messages all around us. We may be drawn to a book or open a page at random and find an answer; meet a person by chance who becomes a catalyst and changes the course of our life forever.

And so it was with Starla-sky

Chapter 1

In the house of lovers, music never stops, the walls are made of songs and the floor dances.
- Rumi -

"Hey – pretty girl!"

Starla-sky stopped dead in her tracks and spun round automatically in the crowded street towards the owner of the voice. People went about their business with indifference.

Unmistakably, the old crone's eyes were fixed straight at her.

"Who - me?" Starla-sky said startled.

"Who else?" spat the old woman. She took a step nearer. "Here – pretty girl. Buy some lucky heather?"

Starla-sky turned on her heels in irritation; her waist length blonde hair swaying like a curtain with the movement.

For her age, the old gypsy was nimble on her feet. Obviously she had no intention of being rebuffed. She caught up with Starla-sky and barred her way.

"I see you in the Andalusian hills," she wailed, her gaze boring intently into Starla-sky's eyes.

"But – but how do you know? I've never seen you before." Starla-sky shivered as if someone had stepped over her grave.

The woman pointed her finger like one possessed and carried on in a shrill voice. "I see you in the hills, dancing away your tragedy, gyrating to guitars – your destiny travelling free under the stars."

In alarm Starla-sky shrank away and sought her escape. The crone shrieked after her.

"Beware, beware – a gold falcon ring and the initial J. Danger awaits you. Listen to me girl!"
Her words were lost amidst the noise of the milling Saturday shoppers and busy traffic as Starla-sky ran blindly back to Raymonde's. It was her last day of employment at the Hairdresser's. She had just finished some last minute shopping in her lunch break for her forthcoming holiday. The bell chimed as she opened the door.

Laura walked out of the staff room, "Are you okay Starla, you look pale?" she inquired, noticing her friend's pallor.

Starla-sky dropped her purchases on the floor and sat down on the chaise longue in the reception area. "I was waylaid by a strange gypsy woman. She gave me a warning – probably because I didn't buy her heather."

Laura's eyes widened. "No tall dark strangers then?" she quipped, finding it highly amusing.

Starla-sky smiled. "Laura you do cheer me up. I'm going to miss you," she replied, before adding. "I'm going to be positive from now on. It's goodbye to the old doormat I had become and good riddance to Matt. I no longer intend to mope around waiting on the end of the phone for him – at his convenience!"

"Good for you Starla. It's about time you came to your senses. I told you that man would never commit, he's too self absorbed." Laura sat down and patted her friend's hand. "You've so much love to give. I so wish you would find someone worthy of you, someone who will love and take care of you. And have eyes for you only!" she stressed, shaking her auburn curls.

Starla-sky took an intake of breath in disbelief. "God, to think I put up with his flirting in front of me. It was totally unacceptable."

"I tried to make you see sense Starla. It's so demeaning and disrespectful. No wonder you were always insecure. He gave you no reason to trust him. A man like that is emotionally degenerate - he needs to get into his heart."

"I know, but he did need his space," Starla-sky said lamely, thinking perhaps she was being a little hard on him.

"C'mon Starla how much space did he need. All those special celebrations like Christmas and New Years Eve. He was never there for you. He wasn't exactly generous either, was he? He never even bought you a birthday present! And don't forget the only time he stayed with you for a whole week was that time he was thrown out of his flat for not paying the rent. Now don't weaken."

"The thing was, he was following some dubious 'spiritual' self styled Guru, who taught nonattachment and freedom."

"Yes to suit men no doubt. I don't know how some people can be so gullible." Laura had always been forthright and could be relied upon to speak her mind regardless. "The way I see nonattachment is not being attached to the outcome of any situation and trusting in the flow of life. Not using it as an excuse to justify selfishness and play with peoples feelings thoughtlessly. Misinterpretation can destroy lives. You have to be so aware to discriminate between these so called spiritual teachers."

"You can be so wise sometimes Laura. You've been such a good friend to me. I don't know what I would have done without your tea and cakes and sympathy."

"That's what best friends are for. I just wish you could meet someone like my Giovanni."

Starla-sky sighed. Laura was so lucky. You could tell by the spring in her step and the song in her voice. But was it luck or was it something else? Starla-sky often wondered and sometimes thought perhaps she herself has chosen to go through this experience for her soul's growth. These deep thoughts came to her occasionally. She never really understood why. Certainly she never shared them with anyone.

"I love the way he's immortalised you in oils." she said.

Giovanni was an Italian artist. From the day he had set eyes on the beautiful Laura with her creamy complexion and smattering of freckles, he was smitten. She said it was love at first sight and now they were inseparable. They were both their number one priority. He called her his titian haired Goddess and couldn't wait to tell the world how proud he was of her. On her birthday he presented her with a heart shaped diamond ring. They were married within the year. There was a positive glow about Laura. It was obvious to everyone they had enhanced each others happiness.

"How long is it now Starla?"

"Four years, can you believe it?" Starla-sky's voice rose with disbelief. "I found out he's been dating Giselle Russell and keeping us both on a string. And God knows who else he's been seeing behind my back. Four years wasted out of my life." Well no more, she thought wryly. The next time he condescends to phone she would be miles away across the sea in Spain. She smiled with amusement imagining his surprise. She owed him nothing after the misery he had put her through.

"Keeping his options open no doubt. What a jerk!" countered Laura. She knew her friend deserved more than the few crumbs he gave her. "He's a shallow, pretentious fool who would never define your relationship. God, Starla, it makes me so mad! You're doing the right thing. If he really cared about you Starla he'd want to share his life with you."

Starla-sky shook her head. "If there's one thing I've learnt it's that I have to take responsibility for my own happiness. I don't need a man to make me happy."

"We'll see about that," said Laura with a knowing look.

Independence had been forced upon Starla-sky from the age of eighteen, to distance herself from her strict Aunt. According to her Aunt Eleanor, Starla-sky's Mother had been the black sheep of the family and had disappeared when Starla-sky was a baby, dumping her almost literally on her doorstep. Her Mother's name was rarely mentioned again. When Starla-sky began asking inquisitive questions, her Aunt revealed that she was the result of a casual fling her mother had indulged in whilst abroad.

Her Aunt's words still rang painfully in her ears. "Your Mother was no good – she never would conform."

Conform to what? Starla-sky had thought sullenly, longing to pluck up the courage to shout at her Aunt, 'To your dogmatic narrow minded ideals, no doubt?'

"No Kirsten was always unconventional," her Aunt had continued, "Travelled with hippies across Spain if you please – said unrealistic nonsense, like she had to search for the spirit of the earth, be close to nature and denounced materialism. And of course you know what those hippies were like – free love and all. Well that's how you came about. God knows who your Father is!"

Starla-sky cringed, recalling the self righteous look on her Aunt's face. It made her feel worthless, as if she should be eternally grateful to her. Aunt Eleanor had brought Starla-sky up accordingly, with unfeeling harsh strictness, to curb any wayward tendencies the girl might have inherited.

Her Aunt was only too pleased when, on her eighteenth birthday, Starla-sky announced she was leaving home. A flat had become available above Raymonde's hairdressers. Aunt Eleanor had practically packed her case for her. As far as she was concerned she had done her duty by Starla-sky and wanted nothing more than to return to the childless state she desired.

Uncle Lawrence on the other hand, was sad to see her go. He was a soft hearted man – long suffering, but nevertheless used to his wife's sharp tongue and loved her in his own way.

Starla-sky couldn't wait to spread her wings and finally do as she pleased. Just be herself without constant criticism. Being young and inexperienced, coming from under her Aunt's sheltered upbringing, her rose tinted specs had yet to be removed.

Matt had come along when she was at her most vulnerable. Feeling suddenly lost and uncertain, the opportunist had appeared like a knight on a white charger. She was soon hopelessly infatuated.

"I can't believe it Laura. This time tomorrow I shall hopefully be lying on soft white sand. It was such a surprise to find I had another Aunt with a hotel in Spain."

"How exactly did you find out?"

"My Aunt Eleanor lost touch with both her sisters. They must have upset her in some way". Starla-sky raised her eyebrows. "It doesn't take much! However, when she discovered her estranged sister had become a wealthy respectable woman, living in a villa in Marbella, she went out of her way for reconciliation."

"How exciting!" exclaimed Laura.

"Hence the invitation for any of us to visit. Aunt Eleanor can't stand the heat, so I'm taking up the offer. Uncle Lawrence was insistent that I should take the opportunity, despite Aunt Eleanor's disapproval."

"For goodness sake! Don't let her bother you," chided Laura.

"Aunt Jessica suggested I come for a holiday and if I decide to stay longer I can help out at their hotel." She knew it was time to move on. Sometimes she thought about Kirsten and sympathised with the way she had felt about life. Aunt Eleanor had a closed mind, she could never understand. Perhaps her Mother's wanderlust ran through her veins.

Laura took hold her by the shoulders and smiled fondly. "Remember, no regrets!"

Starla-sky took a deep breath. "No regrets," she repeated.

"Have a wonderful time," Laura gave her a big hug. "You deserve it Starla-sky."

Early next morning Starla-sky arrived at the airport in drizzling rain. She was not sorry to be leaving for the sun. The flight passed quickly and arrived on schedule at Malaga airport. After collecting her luggage she followed the sign to arrivals. The warm air enveloped her. She blinked in the dazzling sunshine. It was truly like coming out of the dark into the light.

As her eyes became accustomed, she scanned the lounge for a glimpse of her Aunt Jessica. The picture she had in her mind vaguely resembled Aunt Eleanor, tall, severe and statuesque. She was not prepared for the elegant stylish woman approaching her.

"Starla-sky?" The woman inquired hesitantly. "Oh Starla-sky, is it you?" she greeted warmly.

Starla-sky took in the smiling tanned face and short blonde hair. "Yes – are you Aunt Jessica?" she asked with surprise.

"Yes love – but do call me Jessie. Everyone does – except your Aunt Eleanor. My, you are a beauty. I can see you're going to cause quite a stir amongst our local lads," she beamed, and then paused by adding softly. "You remind me so much of Kirsten."

"My Mother?" probed Starla-sky.

"Yes," Aunt Jessie sighed. "Ah – but she's passed away a long time now."

"She's dead!?" exclaimed Starla-sky. Her head began to swim.

"But – yes. Didn't your Aunt Eleanor tell you? I wrote and told her as soon as I knew where she lived. I can't believe she didn't tell you – come and sit down."

Starla-sky looked shocked. How could Aunt Eleanor with hold that information from her? She wondered why she felt so stunned. After all she had never known her Mother. Was she unconsciously expecting to find her on this trip? Was that the real reason she had felt so compelled to come? Did she hope to retrace her Mother's footsteps?

Aunt Jessie beckoned to a man coming through the door. "Over here Federico."

The presence of the stocky Spaniard brought Starla-sky abruptly back to reality.

"Are you alright now dear?" asked Aunt Jessie. "This is Federico my husband. He's brought the car round to the entrance."

"I'm fine." She stood up to shake Federico's hand.

"I am veery pleased to meet you Starla-sky. Welcome to our home," he smiled graciously.

"Thank you," she replied. "So nice to meet you too."

Seated in the comfort of the car's luxurious padded seats Starla-sky's colour began to return.

Aunt Jessie fussed over her. "Eleanor had no right to keep it from you. If I had known I would have waited and broken the news to you when we got to the hotel"

"It's okay. I don't know why I reacted like that?"

"It's understandable. You must rest for the afternoon. We'll have a long talk about it later when you're refreshed."

"I hope you have recovered enough by thees evening," said Federico. "We are having - cabaret at the hotel in celebration. We have the finest singers and flamenco dancers."

"Not for me surely?" Starla-sky looked disconcerted.

"Of course," answered Aunt Jessie. "How often do we get to be reunited with a long lost niece? You'll find Federico likes any excuse to throw a party."

"Your aunt knows me well," said Federico with a chuckle.

In the short time Starla-sky had met him; it was obvious the gentle Spaniard was devoted to her Aunt.

The road west to Marbella followed the shoreline passed numerous attractive beaches. Starla-sky settled back in her seat and considered idly how the place had been aptly named the sunshine coast. She was content to let Aunt Jessie enthuse excitedly as she pointed out places of interest.

"We are coming into Marbella now," informed her Aunt as they passed the well preserved town hall. She pointed to a large section of an impressive castle. "It was built in 960," she nodded.

Starla-sky was suitably inspired as they made their way through the narrow streets to the hotel. Her first impression was one of surprise. The hotel was larger than she imagined and very exclusive.

Aunt Jessie laughed at her bemused expression. "Not what you expected?" she asked. "Federico is a good man. He's worked very hard for this." She pointed to some lavish properties, half hidden by pines. "You see those, they're private clubs – lots of wealth, come by criminally or otherwise, I wouldn't like to say. Our hotel is one of the best. And you can rest assured – I'm proud to say – there is no slur on our reputation."

"It's beautiful."

Starla-sky was taken through an ornate gate into an inner patio enclosed by walls. Large terracotta and earthenware pots lined the stone ground. Flights of steps led to individual balconies, brilliantly whitewashed and enchantingly decorated with a mass of coloured flowers in pots and hanging baskets. The sign 'Hotel Almirante' had pride of place over the entrance.

"I expect you're hungry. When you've freshened up we'll have our lunch. You can rest later," suggested Aunt Jessie. She then called to a young

Spaniard. "Luis – please take my niece's case to the spare room in our quarters."

The boy came over and obligingly lifted the case, grinning widely at Starla-sky. He then acknowledged her Aunt "My pleasure Senora Ramon."

The two women and Federico proceeded to follow him up the stairs. Starla-sky felt weary after her journey, but impatient to talk further to her Aunt about her Mother.

The family quarters consisted of one main living room, small kitchen and three spotless bedrooms with tiled floors and adjoining bathrooms. Aunt Jessie explained that they only make use of these quarters occasionally, spending most of their time at their villa, a few kilometres down the road at Puerto Banus.

"We will be going to the villa after the weekend, so don't unpack yet," she advised.

After settling Starla-sky into the spare room, Aunt Jessie and Federico left her with instructions to meet in the dining hall.

It was mid-day and incredibly hot. She stepped into the bathroom for a quick shower. The rose scent of her shower gel filled the room, awakening her senses. Afterwards she wrapped herself in a large dusty pink towel. The shower had relaxed her, making her feel languorous. She let the towel fall about her feet and applied her rose body lotion with long sensuous strokes. Slipping on her red silk kimono she went into the bedroom to search in her case for something suitable to wear. She went over to the window and looked out. Then stretching her arms to release any tension left in her shoulders; she stopped abruptly, suddenly aware of a presence.

The man stood framed in the doorway. She froze. He eyed her insolently. His dark eyes showed no emotion. She should scream – she should run, but where to? He blocked her only means of escape. His eyes flickered casually over her as she stood rooted to the spot.

In that split second her impression of him was one of pure danger – dangerously ruthless, as if no one could hope to dominate him. Tall and powerfully built, dressed all in black, matching his hair and eyes.

"Excuse - Senorita?" His deep voice cut the atmosphere with a slight American twang. "English?"

She nodded.

"I was looking for Senor Ramon." He spoke with dignity. "He said to come to his quarters. I saw the door ajar and assumed he was here. Let me introduce myself – José Velázquez. I come to dance the flamenco tonight."

"Err - how do you do – Starla-sky Thorson," she stammered mechanically. His presence made her feel uncomfortable.

"Do you know the whereabouts of Senor Ramon?" He asked.

"He should be – by now in the dining hall." She shivered despite the heat.

"Gracias." He turned on his heels, and then glanced back at her. "If I were you I would keep this door shut."

Voices from below in the courtyard jolted Starlasky out of her state of shock. Removing the tortoiseshell clamp, she allowed her hair to tumble luxuriantly around her shoulders. She dressed hurriedly in a short primrose embroidery anglais sundress and espadrilles. Composing herself she took a deep breath and headed for the dining hall.

Chapter 2

The bar was crowded with tourists. By their voices she noted the majority were English. She caught sight of Federico. José Velázquez was leaning nonchalantly against the bar listening courteously to the older man. His eyes wandered lazily around the room, and settled on Starla-sky. She hurried on to the dining hall.

"Starla-sky dear – over here." Aunt Jessie was waving to attract her attention.
"Now what would you like to eat?"
"What do you suggest?"
"I think you will like Gazpacho, a refreshing cold soup, to start. And then fish fries and salad."
"Will Federico be joining us?"
"No he's talking business in the bar. He is tactfully leaving us to lunch alone."

Starla-sky looked thoughtfully at her Aunt. The waiter came to take their order.

"I can't understand why Eleanor didn't tell you about your Mother," said Aunt Jessie angrily. "She can be so insensitive."

"Well she speaks highly of you at present. She was most impressed with your letter."

"Oh – what a wonderful thing it is to be approved by Eleanor," laughed Aunt Jessie. "I suppose I'm respectable enough for her now."

Aunt Jessie was so unlike her Aunt Eleanor, thought Starla-sky. She was warm, witty and attractive. It was easy to like her.

"Please tell me what happened to my Mother?"

Aunt Jessie leaned forward. "It was a strange coincidence how I found out. You see it was five years after her death that I heard the news." She unfolded her napkin, and then continued. "Federico and I were sitting in a local café. A man happened to be passing through. We got talking. He was quite a story teller – bit of a traveller. He said that due to an accident he had now slowed down." Aunt Jessie stopped and looked sympathetically at Starla-sky. "I noticed his face was badly scarred and inquired what happened."

Starla-sky went cold.

"He looked sad as if it had preyed on his mind for years. I apologised and said if he would rather not talk about it… But he insisted. It all came pouring out how he had picked up a hitch hiker – he'd met her briefly once before." Aunt Jessie hesitated and then continued. "I'm sorry dear what I'm about to tell you. But you have a right to know."

"Yes – yes, Aunt Jessie – go on," implored Starla-sky.

"The motor bike came roaring out of a side turning, like a bat out of hell. The brunt of the impact – the girl – was killed instantly and he sustained head injuries – thrown though the windscreen… He was visibly shaken recalling the accident when he mumbled, 'Poor Kirsten.' Kirsten? I said with growing concern. Then he went on to describe her appearance and sweet nature. She told him she had gone home to England to give birth to her baby girl. She'd had to leave her there with her sister for awhile and return urgently to

Spain for some reason. She seemed very sad. He didn't like to pry any further."

Starla-sky took a sharp intake of breath and gripped the table. "Oh no," she gasped.

"I then contacted the Spanish authorities and they confirmed my worst fears. They had not been able to trace any relatives." Aunt Jessie reached her hand across the table to Starla-sky. "Apparently your Mother had some obscure address on her passport, where she had once lived."

Starla-sky listened intently. Aunt Jessie took a spoonful of her soup. "This is good – try some," she urged.

Starla-sky lifted her spoon. "What was she like – my Mother?"

Aunt Jessie smiled. "I guess Kirsten was a free spirit."

"Aunt Eleanor said she was the black sheep of the family."

"I can well imagine how Eleanor described her! I was the one who was close to Kirsten. We were both rebelling in those days against our middle class background."

"Did you travel to Spain together?"

Aunt Jessie smiled, "Yes we were following the Hippie movement. We weren't consciously aware then that unseen forces were urging us on. I later studied Astrology you see. The Hippie movement came from the stars literally. In 1965 there was a rare conjunction of Uranus and Pluto. It brought sudden changes, freedom, and transformation. It was a time of revolution and spiritual growth. Venus brought the true nature of universal love. It was indeed our summer of love. I'm not surprised she named you Starla-sky – child from the stars."

Starla-sky put her spoon down. "Oh my God really?" She looked at her Aunt and felt a deep empathy. "That's so interesting I often wondered where it came from. Aunt Eleanor could never understand why my Mother had given me that 'weird' name, as she called it. I seem to remember she wanted to change it but Uncle Lawrence for once put his foot down. He somehow felt my mother would not abandon me and insisted on keeping her choice for my name."

"It's a lovely choice. Thank goodness for Uncle Lawrence." Aunt Jessie leaned forward and continued. "When we came here we found a deeper need for human nature. We left behind the organised rigid lifestyle which is expected of us for a higher standard of living. This land nourishes a sense of poetry which is far removed from the materialist pursuit."

"So – when did you lose touch with my Mother?"

Aunt Jessie sighed. "Kirsten was forever searching for the intangible. I knew I had to let her go. She was unique. I think, somehow, far advanced from us spiritually. She could see things we couldn't"

Starla-sky's eyes were moist. "I can't tell you how wonderful it is to hear all this about my Mother. I somehow feel I've found her. It makes me feel so worthwhile. Aunt Eleanor said she was permissive."

"Oh did she now! That sister of mine has a poisoned mind. I can assure you Kirsten was far from permissive. She was aware of how detrimental that could be spiritually; and how each intimate encounter can imprint in our aura for years and affect us in adverse ways. She believed in soul mates."

"I believe my Father was her soul mate." She somehow knew it was true.

. "Yes – I'm sure," Aunt Jessie looked thoughtful. "It's a mystery why he never claimed you – there must be a good reason."

"Perhaps we'll never know," Starla-sky stated soberly. "Did she look like me?"

"You are very like her – same blonde hair and blue eyes. Perhaps her hair was even lighter than yours. Her skin was so pale it was almost translucent." Aunt Jessie smiled and tilting her head, studied Starla-sky closely. "Yes – your eyes are more cobalt blue – nearly navy and your nose more aquiline. You have certainly inherited the Thorson's flaxen hair. Father always insisted our ancestors were Vikings."

"Really? Aunt Eleanor never…"

"Mentioned it – I know," interrupted Aunt Jessie. "She would have pooh-poohed the very idea. As far as she was concerned, she considered herself an upstanding English lady. Anyone south of Dover was a foreigner and not to be trusted."

Starla-sky giggled. How extremely well Aunt Jessie knew her Aunt Eleanor. It was odd and enlightening sitting here talking about her like this. Starla-sky was so glad she had made the decision to come to Spain. She felt a great weight lifted from her shoulders, as if a ghost had finally been laid to rest. A sense of optimism – even excitement rushed through her veins.

After lunch they retired to their separate rooms for siesta. Starla-sky found it difficult to sleep. Her mind was racing with all the new information she had absorbed. Eventually she dozed off and didn't stir until it was time for the evening meal. Sleepily she opened her eyes and for a moment was disorientated. Glancing at the clock she gasped and swung her legs out of bed. There wasn't much time. She didn't want to be late.

The flamenco dancers had arrived and were talking raucously in the hotel dressing room. Federico was trying without success to gain order.

"Trankeelo! Por favor," he urged.

Nobody paid any attention. Loud conversation in some obscure dialect drowned his attempts.

Suddenly a deep authorative voice broke through the din. The reaction was immediate – complete hush descended throughout the room. The owner of the voice was a man of extraordinary presence. All eyes were on him. It was José Velázquez!

Starla-sky arrived in the dining hall with minutes to spare. She had been undecided about what to wear – her black dress or loose white trousers and halter neck top. After hurriedly trying on both, she chose the strapless dress in soft cotton Lycra. Eyes turned in admiration towards her as she passed by the tables.

She was conscious of the paleness of her skin compared to the tanned tourists who had obviously worked hard to acquire their deep mahogany bronze. Her dress, just above her knees, showed of her perfectly shaped legs. Aunt Jessie was seated at a front table close to the stage. Guitarists were tuning their instruments to snatches of 'Guantanamera,' the strains of the music setting the atmosphere for the evening.

Apparently satisfied with their sound, they continued the gentle rhythm of the verse. Starla-sky joined her Aunt at the table. Aunt Jessie was dressed in pale turquoise. The raw silk two piece, embossed with tiny Spanish flowers, complimented her golden tan. Starla-sky thought she looked radiant.

"Hello Aunt Jessie, hope you haven't been waiting long."

"No dear," her Aunt smiled. "I didn't like to wake you."

"I feel revived now." Starla-sky's eyes sparkled with renewed energy.

"When Federico arrives we'll eat and after dinner we can enjoy the flamenco."

Starla-sky tapped her fingers to the rhythm of the Spanish music. The guitarists were singing now, their voices rising in crescendo.

Federico arrived with the waiter. "So sorry to keep you waiting ladees. I have been trying to calm the flamenco dancers – so volatile – impossseeble. Such dramatics. Thank God for José Velázquez. His strength is indomitable. They look to him for guidance. A man proud of his origins. No ordinary Spanish gypsy!"

"Gypsy?" echoed Starla-sky. "Is José Velázquez a gypsy?"

"Si – I find them the best dancers – pure flamenco," answered Federico with elation.

"What's the difference?"

"Ah – take my word for it." He raised his eyes heavenward. "The pito, the palmada – the taconeo. They dance without pillillos. Wait and see."

"Pillillos?" inquired Starla-sky.

"Castanets," answered Aunt Jessie. "They don't use them – just finger snapping – or castanuela's, to mark the rhythm. And hand clapping. Taconeo is a form of fast tap dancing."

Whilst enjoying paella and sangria with the lilting melody of singing in the background, Aunt Jessie and Federico explained the fundamentals of flamenco.

Presently, much to Starla-sky's surprise, one of the guitarists left the stage and walked slowly past the tables, stopping to serenade her. She smiled politely. The waiter then reappeared to take their plates and refill the empty sangria jug. Pleasantly relaxed, she sat back in her seat and sipped her drink.

The song concluded, Federico clapped his hands enthusiastically. "Bravo Miguel!"

The guitarist bowed his head, and then returned to the stage to rejoin his fellow musicians. With a great flourish, the whole group bowed deeply and then disappeared backstage, only to return again a few seconds later as accompaniment to the dancers. As the music increased in intensity, four women spun wildly across the stage, their feet tapping in mock passion and pirouettes, causing their brightly coloured flounced skirts to rise provocatively.

White teeth flashed against deep olive skin – sleek black patent hair, thickly plaited and coiled securely at the nape of their necks.

A young man about mid twenties entered the centre of the women. Heel clicking, hands clapping, his face expressed profound emotion. Starla-sky was surprised to see he had blonde hair, but his skin was nut brown like the women. He wore a jet black outfit with a gold embroidered waistcoat.

He stamped his feet, glanced at the audience and smiled broadly at Starla-sky. She was impressed. His gaze left her abruptly as a petite dancer with large liquid eyes came tap-tapping across the stage. She smiled as she reached the man. Her red and black tiered skirt swayed in harmony as she circled him. It was beautiful to watch. The audience grew less tense, quickly becoming enraptured.

Suddenly the calm was broken by the entrance of another striking beauty. The music changed dramatically, consumed with passion. The dancer's expressive dark eyes flashed, darting back and forth from the audience to the guitarists. Large gold hoops glinted, half hidden by her wild mane of tousled hair. Encouraged by the cries from the guitarists and other dancers she was stimulated into a state of tempestuous frenzy. At the height of her excitement she stopped briefly, smoothing her hands down over her hips, waiting for her partner.

Starla-sky's heart missed a beat as José Velázquez made his entrance with all the drama of an untamed animal come for the kill. One arm encircling the woman's waist, he stood in arrogance, eyes fixed somewhere at the back of the room. All the passion, torment and deep expressive qualities of a people who have known the effects of a turbulent geography were mirrored in his face.

As he began dancing the audience clapped in time to his thundering heels. Starla-sky was transfixed. For some reason he deeply disturbed her. An unreasonable fear gripped her. He had an awesome presence. The way he danced hypnotised her – almost an element of being under his possession.

At the end of the dance she sighed with relief. The audience stood clapping rapturously, while the pair took their bow. Shouts of 'encore, encore' were heard above the noise. More and more people started shouting, until the guitars began playing again, and the performers began tapping their feet once more.

José Velázquez and his partner disappeared out the back. The dancers were now in good spirits and teased the audience, daring them to join them on the stage. The blonde man came down towards Starla-sky, and before she realised what was happening, he had hold of her hand and was pulling her up. He proceeded to dance around her, and then invited her to follow.

"Tap your feet Senorita," he urged.

She obliged and found the steps not as easy as it looked. He laughed at her brave attempts and she laughed with him.

"You are – how you say – good sport," he grinned.

By then she was not alone. Aunt Jessie and a few other women and a man had also been hauled up to dance. Starla-sky was enjoying herself. She liked the young man instantly. First impressions were not always correct, she had found, much to her detriment, but in this case she was sure she would not be proved wrong.

"How long did it take you to learn flamenco?" she asked as he guided her through the steps.

"I've been dancing all my life. It is my life!" he answered intensely and then asked. "You like?"

"Yes – I like," she smiled.

"Let me teach you then," he suggested. "I think you are a natural."

"I don't know…" she began

"Sure you do. Look – I'm staying in Marbella for a few days. My name is Paco Herrera – and you are Starla, Federico Ramon's niece." He clapped his hands. "Si I know all about you."

Starla-sky smiled, she could not take offence to his forthright manner. His face was too open. "You speak good English," she said.

"Si – my Mother - English. She taught my people."

"I suppose that also accounts for your blonde hair."

"Si – that is so. I have not been to England. Perhaps you could tell me about it?"

"Perhaps I could," she ventured. "Hasn't your Mother told you about England?

"Some," he answered.

The music came to a pause and Federico jumped up onto the stage. He praised the dancers, and then called. "Uno momento! Uno momento! Ladees and Gentlemen, I would like to say a few words of welcome to my wife's beautiful niece, Starla-sky. It is wonderful surprise to meet her finally." He beckoned her over. "Come! Come!"

She gulped, and then joined him, smiling graciously.

"Let us raise our glasses and drink a toast. May she enjoy our glorious country – Starla-sky!"

Everyone cheered. Through her embarrassment Starla-sky felt a pleasant warmth envelope her. Aunt Jessie joined them and put her arm around her. A lump came to Starla-sky's throat and all she could manage was an emotional – "Thank you."

Federico threw his hands up. "Let the dancing commence!"

On cue, the guitarists began strumming a lively tune. Paco grabbed Starla-sky by the hand and led her down from the stage to dance. This prompted others to follow and soon a whole crowd filled the dance floor.

"Now you can teach me," said Paco. "You dance the disco well."

"Thank you. But you're not doing too badly," she enthused.

"No, I am more trained for flamenco. But this is fun."

"It is – but I think your dancers are superb. Flamenco is much harder to learn I should think."

"Well – my offer still stands." He raised an eyebrow.

Much to her surprise she found herself replying. "Okay – you're on."

Chapter 3

The evening was a great success. Wine flowed freely, the mood was merry, and all inhibitions were lost. Starla-sky noticed the flamenco dancers gathered together in a group, watching the dancing and drinking sangria. Paco's exquisite little dancing partner had been claimed by a tall German and appeared to be enjoying herself twirling to the music.

Between dances, Paco insisted on introducing Starla-sky to the group. He reeled off their names, "Carita – Monolita – Isabel – Anna…"

As they nodded polite greetings, Starla-sky felt the gypsy reserve. Paco quickly moved on to the dark eyed fiery looking girl who had partnered José Velázquez. She was sitting at a table talking in Spanish to an English man.

"This is Marcia," informed Paco. "She cannot speak English." He then spoke to the girl in his native tongue. Starla-sky heard him mention her name. Marcia lifted her chin to look her up and down. It was an icy cold stare; the faintest of smiles curved her lips. Starla-sky could sense the girl's hostility. The eyes said it all. She spoke with them – crossed languages.

The man seated beside her rose and offered his hand to Starla-sky. "Johnny Spears," he nodded.

Starla-sky went to extend her arm, and then shrank back in alarm at the sight of his outstretched hand. A silver ring gleamed on his little finger. As it shone under the artificial lighting, she noticed the outline of a raised falcon. He was dressed in an expensive Italian suit, but his straggly greased back hair betrayed his true character. Aunt Eleanor would have said he was a wide boy or spiv.

It was all Starla-sky could do to stop herself from shaking as she forced herself to be polite. Why was she behaving so strangely? It was only a coincidence. Nobody in their right mind would believe the ramblings of an old crone in a London street, she thought rationally. She steeled herself to shake his hand.

"From England eh love?" he asked. "Whereabouts?"

"London," she replied. She wanted to go. She didn't want to stand here making conversation with this man. They would think her unsociable, but she didn't care. There was something unsavoury about him.

Paco must have felt her unease, for he guided her back onto the dance floor as the music began playing 'Viva Espana.'

Soon her unexplained fears were forgotten and the evening progressed light heartedly. It ended agreeably with Paco making arrangements to meet her on the beach at Puerto Banus the next day. They were to discuss her visit to the gypsy encampment, where Paco would teach her the flamenco.

Later, back in her room, she wondered whether the sangria had made her abandon her senses. It was a reckless thing to agree to. These were wild gypsies, she knew nothing about. They could be murderers or thieves for all she knew. After all, did gypsies not have the reputation for being a law unto themselves? She had always been led to believe they were dangerous and to be avoided. But no, Paco didn't fit that image at all. He had proved himself a convivial companion tonight with his boyish charm. He wasn't that much older than her, she reckoned.

Then of course there was José Velázquez! Now, he was different. And where had he so mysteriously disappeared to tonight, she wondered? It was not as if she cared of course. It was mere curiosity. If he didn't want to stay to enjoy the evening, that was his choice. Anyway his presence may have dampened her pleasure.

She was pleasantly tired as she stepped out of her dress and discarded it carelessly onto the chair. It was far too hot to wear anything at all in bed tonight. Thankfully slipping between the crisp cotton sheets she fell into a peaceful sleep.

The next morning she opened her eyes to the sun streaming through the Venetian blinds, she had forgotten to close the previous night. Instinctively, she blinked and shaded her eyes with her hand, before grabbing her robe and jumping out of bed. Sounds drifted up from downstairs. The hotel staff had already started their day. She looked out of the window. The bright sunshine bathed the whiteness of the buildings below. The swimming pool could just be seen glittering lustrously to her left.

A couple appeared to be taking an early morning dip. The girl, clad in a tiny bikini, ran along the edge of the pool, shrieking gleefully as the boy chased her, until they collapsed together into the water. Starla-sky sighed, how happy they looked, like carefree lovers. For a fleeting moment envy crossed her mind. She dismissed the thought abruptly. She was not going to keep thinking any more 'if only.' Anyway today she was going swimming with Paco and intended to enjoy herself.

She glanced at the clock. It was eight thirty, later than she thought, but not too late for breakfast. There was just time for a quick shower, before going downstairs. She checked that she had locked the door last night; not wanting a repeat performance of yesterday's episode. It was highly unlikely José Velázquez would be around the hotel today as the whole troupe of dancers had left. But she was not taking any chances.

After her shower she slipped on denim shorts and sun top over her blue polka dot bikini. She went downstairs for croissants and coffee. Aunt Jessie and Federico were already busy organising the staff. She finished her coffee and said she would be back later.

Once outside into the sunshine, Starla-sky put on her sunglasses and made her way up the quaint winding street to the bus stop. Dawdling slowly past the market, she cast her eyes over the brightly coloured embroidered clothes, miniature pictures and local pottery for sale. The scorching sun stinging her back, made her hurry on reluctantly. She could, quite happily, have browsed for hours. Luckily the bus was waiting in the square. She paid the driver and sat down at an open window. The breeze from the moving vehicle was a welcome relief.

Alighting at Puerto Banus, she strolled past little boutiques along the promenade. Large yachts in the marina were grouped together lining the sea wall. A middle aged man of affluent appearance glanced up as Starla-sky approached. His expression showed slight interest. He then turned back to his companion, who was lazing on the deck in swimming shorts. Coming level, she recognised him as the man she had met last night – Johnny Spears. She fixed her gaze straight ahead and walked hastily on to the beach.

Paco was already swimming in the clear blue water. The little flamenco dancer he had partnered last night was playfully splashing him. Starla-sky took off her sandals and walked across the sand. It was so hot; she hurried to find a spot to lay her towel to sit on. She watched the pair in the sea, feeling a little intrusive. The girl wore a one piece black swimsuit, although plain it accented her perfectly proportioned petite figure. She was daintily pretty in the delicate boned gitana way. Paco lifted her up into his arms laughing, and then dropped her back into the sea. She squealed with obvious delight. He looked towards the beach and Starla-sky waved. He waved back, swam to the edge and ran towards her. The girl followed.

"Glad you made it," he panted, and then introduced the girl. "This is Anita. She wanted to meet you – she didn't get the chance last night."

"Hi!" Anita said breathlessly, "nice to meet you."

Starla-sky noticed Anita had that slight American lilt to her voice, like José Velázquez. "I did enjoy your dancing last night it was fantastic!" she enthused.

"Gracias. It is a wonderful dance our people have handed down for centuries," Anita smiled. "So – Paco is to teach you?"

"Yes – I hope so," said Starla-sky apprehensively. Although Anita was so gentle and friendly, Starla-sky's intuition prompted the uncanny feeling that the girl regretted Paco's offer. Perhaps her imagination was working overtime, for Anita smiled sweetly, her heart shaped face creasing into dimples in her cheeks.

"Come for a swim. The waters warm." Anita ran off like an excited child towards the sea.

"Wait a second," called Starla-sky, slipping off her shorts and top.

Paco ran on ahead. Starla-sky joined them. There was no need to ease her way in like she did back home in England. There, it was often icy cold. Here, she drifted in backwards, enjoying the luxury of the warm ocean. She swam alongside them, joining in their laughter and joking easy going manner.

Starla-sky was the first to leave the water to relax on her towel. Five minutes later Paco joined her, leaving Anita playing with some young children who had gathered in the shallows. Starla-sky watched them with interest.

"Anita is pretty," she remarked.

"Yes," murmured Paco.

"Why does she speak with an American accent?" Starla-sky's curiosity had got the better of her. "The dark man - José Velázquez does also."

"Si –Anita is the little sister of José."

"Really?" Starla-sky jerked her head towards him in surprise.

He continued. "They both lived in America for awhile. Their parents and brothers are still there."

"I see. What made them return?"

"This place is in their blood Starla. José had no intention of staying for good in America."

"And Anita?"

"Anita also – she begged José to bring her back with him. But she is young. She doesn't know her own mind. After tasting the modern way of life in America, she will probably want to return." He looked down soberly and kicked at the sand. "The gypsies could never be enough for her – it stands to reason – the novelty will soon wear off and she will tire of us."

"Not necessarily," answered Starla-sky, sensing his despondency. "What made the family go anyway?"

"Many years ago, as a young boy, José's uncle left for California. He made his fortune and on a visit home persuaded José's Father to go back with him, leaving José's Mother behind. Each time his Father returned, his Mother bore a son – until José was born – the seventh son, and then Anita the youngest. Eventually they all joined their Father in the States to be educated. They accompanied their mother on the long voyage. But José had the calling to return home and help his people."

Starla-sky sat silently thoughtful, musing over this information about the mysterious José Velázquez.

Paco paused for awhile, sifting his fingers through the sand, and then added. "So far we have managed to open the children's school."

"That's wonderful Paco."

"It was José's consistent hard work that initiated it. I take the English lessons with the young ones – and of course the flamenco, which is second nature to us."

"You have a full life Paco. Do you live far from here?" she asked.

"We live in the foothills of the Sierra Nevada Mountains – in the caves on the outskirts of Granada."

"When will you be going home?"

"The day after tomorrow. Anita will return with me. José is seeing to some business in Marbella today."

"I expect he's impatient to get back also."

"He does have a lot to attend to," said Paco, and then grinned. "He also likes to unwind and enjoy himself."

"You could have fooled me," blurted Starla-sky impulsively...

"What do you mean?"

"Well – he didn't stay long last night did he?"

Paco glanced at her sideways. "After a performance, he finds the disco too much. You have to understand him."

She didn't think she would ever understand such an impenetrable man.

"You must come on Friday to our camp for the weekend, and I can begin to teach you the flamenco," he enthused. "Take the bus from Malaga. I will meet you at Granada."

"Okay," she answered slowly. What on earth had she let herself in for? They lived in caves for God's sake!

Anita came running up the beach, with a line of giggling children in tow. She looked radiant, laughing and swinging her long plait. She planted herself breathlessly onto her towel, the children jumping up and down beside her.

"Say hi to my friends, Paco and Starla-sky," she said to them in Spanish.

They all shrieked in unison. "Hi Paco – Starry-skies, starry-skies," and then collapsed giggling in a heap.

"This is Chico, Tonita and Miguel," informed Anita. "I've been teaching them some English words."

Starla-sky smiled. "Hello," she said. They were indeed enchanting – huge brown eyes and dark brown hair, the little girl's face framed by a mass of curls – all brown as berries.

Paco began blowing up the beach ball. "Who wants to play catch?" he asked.

Three little voices chimed. "Me! Me! Me!"

Anita jumped up again. "Come, I'll play."

Such energy, thought Starla-sky. Anita can't sit still for a moment.

"Catch Starla," shouted Paco. There was no question of them allowing her to laze on her towel.

Soon she was enjoying the game as much as them. It was late afternoon before they said their goodbyes.

"We hope to see you at the disco tonight Starla," said Paco. "It's at the hotel Calypso."

"Okay. I'll see you there," she answered as she left them.

Later, as Starla-sky showered ready for the evening, she winced with pain. The day on the beach had left her sunburnt. She would have to wear something cool, and that meant not much at all, she conceded. Her cream bustier teamed with a tobacco coloured short skirt would be most suitable, she decided.

Once dressed, she sat by the mirror to apply a little enhancing makeup. She had always been told that her eyes were her most expressive feature. She applied some iridescent eye shadow in copper, highlighted with sunburst. Then added a fine line of kohl, a coat of mascara and brushed on a light dusting of golden bronze loose powder to tone her skin down. She completed the look with a touch of sheer lip gloss to complement her flamboyantly shaded eyes.

The last time she went to a disco, she recalled Matt frantically applying hair gel in front of the mirror – slapping on too much after shave, and then agonising over whether his shirt was the correct shade to match his trousers. She was blind to how infuriatingly vain he could be. She had been in love, or so she thought. How foolish she was and how surprisingly short the euphoria had lasted.

Slipping into her strappy heels she grabbed her bag and went.

A short walk down the steps and across the square brought her to the centre of the town. The lively beat of guitars could already be heard coming from the hotel Calypso. White tables and chairs spilled out onto the street, filled with laid back tourists, set to enjoy themselves. A number of Spaniards occupied an end table. Paco was amongst them. His boyish face creased into a grin.

"You look simpatico – very nice Starla." He acknowledged.

"Nice?" she teased.

"That's a compliment!"

She smiled. It was good to see him. Anita was already on the centre of the dance floor when they entered. She danced vivaciously, her movements' quick and lithe, snake- like. With sheer exuberance she rippled like a contortionist, to the point of nearly slipping out of her skimpy red vest dress. Her black hair hung loose to one side, clasped with an exotic crimson flower.

Paco bought Starla-sky a drink. A laser beam flashed silver about the room, spinning lights, casting shadows, distorting the dancing figures. Starla-sky joined Anita on the dance floor. They spun to the music, their hair contrasting dramatically under the glowing light.

It was not long before they were surrounded by a crowd of Spanish boys, desperately intent on competing, who could dance the wildest. Starla-sky was enjoying all the attention. It had been a long time since she had let her hair down and was finding it pleasurable. Her face lit animatedly. A sense of frivolity made her return the smiles of the boys. She was flirting, and she knew it – and she didn't care.

It was innocent fun, nobody was taking it seriously; except, for one man standing in the corner who was staring at her with a stony expression. Twirling around, she caught his eye as the lights flashed.

It surprised her to see him here. José Velázquez was not one for discos, she thought. The beautiful Marcia stood close to his side, her dark eyes resting on him possessively. They somehow looked innocuously out of place. He, dressed carelessly in black, as if he couldn't be bothered to co-ordinate different colours. And Marcia still appeared to be dressed in her flamenco costume. Starla-sky could not begin to imagine José Velázquez preening himself in front of a mirror with hair gel, let alone use after shave. She giggled at the mere thought. His expression was growing colder by the minute. She suppressed another giggle.

A few moments later, Anita saw him also and threw her arms in the air excitedly. "José – José." She called, and ran over to him.

Anita then proceeded to drag him onto the dance floor, leaving a sullen Marcia. He looked extremely reluctant to begin with, but soon yielded to his little sister's quick witted lively coercing. Much to Starla-sky's astonishment, he showed himself to be a competent dancer. The disco was not that alien to him after all.

The music died to a slow number. Anita whispered in José's ear before joining Paco. Much to Starla-sky's surprise José Velázquez grabbed hold of her.

"My little sister thinks we should dance together – if you are agreeable?"

"Why not?" she answered, flippantly.

"I do not usually frequent the discos," he said arrogantly. "I come to keep an eye on my sister tonight."

"I am sure she will be fine." She gave him a reassuring smile.

"She is no more than an impressionable child," he countered. "The foreign tourists have invaded our shores with their permissive ways."

"That's a bit strong!"

His eyes wandered over her insolently. He raised an eyebrow and commented. "You are foolish to sit in the sun so long. Such delicate skin."

Was he mocking her? "Maybe I did overdo it today. It was my first time on the beach." She wished he would just lighten up.

As the dance came to an end, he escorted her back to her seat. "Gracias Senorita," He looked straight into her eyes and kissed her hand.

She took a sharp intake of breath. Her pulse began to beat wildly, making it difficult to speak. She had never met a man like him before. Against her will, he frightened and excited her.

Nonchantly, he made his way back to an irate Marcia. Starla-sky took a long sip of her drink to steady her nerves. As the music started up again, Paco asked her to dance. Gliding across the floor, they almost bumped into José and Marcia.

Marcia fastened her gaze deliberately on Starla-sky with undisguised jealous hostility. If looks could kill! She thought. Surely Marcia didn't think she was interested in José? No way José, she quipped inwardly.

"Enjoying yourself?" Paco cut into her thoughts.

"Yes - I suppose the evening is nearly over. It's very late."

"It is time for the last dance," he answered. "You do not mind if I partner Anita?"

"Of course not Paco. I've had enough anyway." She laughed, "I'm dead on my feet."

The music stopped. Paco thanked her and went in search of Anita. Starla-sky was just about to collapse onto a chair, when a strong arm boldly encircled her waist. "Senorita - I would like this dance!" José Velázquez was insistent.

"I think you should dance with Marcia," she replied.

"No – she is dancing with someone," he informed her.

Paco and Anita beckoned to them from the dance floor. Before she could protest, Jose had whisked her across the floor to join them.

He held her firmly. Adrenalin coursed through her veins, making her heart pound.

"Ah, now this is my kind of music," he murmured seductively in her ear."

She suddenly felt light headed. He was holding her too close.

"I have been watching you - you move well. You have sensuous rhythm," he breathed.

The electricity that surged through her, like a bolt of lightening, shocked and confused her. His fingers found hers. She recalled something she had once read, about sudden unexplained chemistry that can happen between the most unlikely strangers. The last thing she wanted was to feel aroused like this. She did not want to fall in love again – ever, or at least, not with such an unfathomable man.

He held her tighter. Had he felt her response? She stiffened. The closeness of his body was overpowering. She quivered weakly against him. The music ended. He loosened his grip and looked down at her. He held her at arms length, took a bow and without a word turned on his heels.

Starla-sky was speechless. If she was honest he had stirred tumultuous feelings from deep within her. Matt had never had this electrifying affect on her. No – he had charmed her when it suited him, then provoked her by acting cold and distant. He had never had a sensual presence. She could not deny the basic animal magnetism that attracted her to José Velázquez. But God, she would fight it all the way!

Chapter 4

The bus from Malaga slowly wound its way inland, past sparsely populated villages, taking Starla-sky on her journey to Granada. It was a new experience for her. She gazed out over dead straight lines of vineyards and orchards, praised by Arab poets for the fine wines which they yielded. Females working in the fields could be seen, dressed in long cotton clothes to shield them from the relentless shining sun.

Paco and Anita had returned home to the caves. And José…? Yes him also. But Starla-sky didn't want to think about him. The man was arrogant and she had the impression that he held the opinion that women were inferior. There was no place in her affections for a man like that.

She reminded herself of the resolution she had made when she left England. Not to be taken on the downhill roller-coaster of desire and deceit, was firmly etched in her mind. She was now immune to the silly emotions he had aroused in her that night.

She was feeling adventurous. It was time to explore. Any fears she had felt when agonising over her impulsiveness were soon put to rest by Aunt Jessie and Federico.

"Go by all means," Aunt Jessie had said. "It's a wonderful opportunity."

"Si – we know Paco well," said Federico. "He will protect you. Si – guard you with his life. No one dare harm you – have great honour for amigos, these gypsies."

"Yes, you are honoured. Not many tourists would be allowed to enter their territory," said Aunt Jessie. "Let alone teach their treasured flamenco."

Early afternoon, the heat was intense, relieved only by the slight breeze coming from the open window at the front of the bus. Starla-sky fanned her face with her magazine. She would have preferred to travel later in the day, but Paco had insisted she did not travel alone in the evening. It was sweet of him to be so protective, but she was quite capable of taking care of herself. Still, she didn't want to offend him.

The driver turned to face the passengers, who were mostly elderly English tourists. The bus continued doggedly on, as if it was so familiar with the journey, it knew its own way.

"We are soon to enter the town of Granada," he informed them in very good practised English. "We will keep to the main road. The valleys would be quicker route to take, but some are very narrow and the spacious valleys are difficult to access." He then turned his attention back to the road ahead, to the relief of the passengers.

In the distance Starla-sky could see the shimmering town in the foothills of the Sierra Nevada Mountains, built on and around the three hills of the Albaicin, Sacromente and Alhambra. She had this strange feeling of de je vu. Closing her eyes, pictures darted across her mind. Her head was full of flights of fancy and fountains – Cypress and lemon trees, amongst fern-like foliage – and cascading blossoms – reflections in springs with rose and water lilies. It was like the Garden of Eden, surrounding a magical palace with echoing alleyways. When she opened her eyes again the bus had come to a halt.

Alighting at Granada, there was no sign of Paco. Starla-sky stopped under the shade of an oleander tree to wait. As an attractive English girl alone, she stood out in her fashionable purple seashell print halter top and matching sarong skirt. Her hair hung to her waist in a single plait.

A group of scruffy little boys suddenly appeared from out of nowhere. "Americano? Inglis?" they asked. "I take you on tour," one said. He looked at her with shrewd eyes far advanced than his years, as if he had seen it all a hundred times before. He continued to tell her his well rehearsed facts. "Si – in 711 the Moors invaded Granada and soon conquered all of Espana. In 1492 their final stronghold, Granada, fell to the advancing Reyes Catolicos, Ferdinand and Isobel. The city was named after Grana, daughter of Noah. Or some claim Granata, daughter of Hercules. Si – come. How much you pay?"

"No, I am meeting someone," she interrupted swiftly and went to walk away. She hoped Paco had not forgotten to meet her.

This did not deter the boy who followed close on her heels. "He not come – stood you up," he informed her with indifference; immune to it all.

"Starla-sky!"

The sound of her name being called filled her with relief. Thank goodness, Paco was rescuing her from further harassment.

"Over here!" he yelled brusquely.

The boys disappeared in a flash, de-materialising before her eyes.

As she spun round, she saw with alarm, it was not Paco, but José Velázquez in an old jeep.

Reluctantly, she walked over to him. "But – I am waiting for Paco," she scowled ungratefully.

His black eyes flickered casually over her. He looked bored. "He is busy preparing for the dancing tonight – so I have come for you." He spoke as if she was some tiresome child, and then reached across and opened the door for her.

There was no alternative but to get in. "Is it far?" she inquired haughtily.

"A fair way," he answered, and then starting the jeep, he roared off almost before she had time to sit down.

"You didn't have to come you know," she said, when she had resigned herself to the inevitable and adjusted to his erratic driving.

"And who else is there to collect you?" he replied. A sardonic smile played about his lips. "Do your talents go beyond disco dancing to – perhaps flying?"

She had the urge to slap him, but controlled herself. "You'd be surprised what other talents I have," she snapped angrily.

"No – I have no doubt." His eyes glanced fleetingly over her. "I would be blind not to be aware of your obvious - talents."

She seethed. What was he insinuating?

They had been travelling well away from the town. The gypsy caves were on the road to Sacromente, to the east, beyond the Albaicin, from

San Miguel to the Darro valley. On its right, further to the east were the white washed entrances to the gypsy caves.

After their first unfortunate clash of personalities, Starla-sky had no wish to converse further and contented herself with admiring the scenery. He was silent also, his mind rock hard, she suspected; a man of few words.

She assessed his profile. Swarthy aquiline features set in a face – yes – his face was disturbingly handsome. What was she doing anyway… about to be mesmerised by his clear carved bone structure?

They came to a slight hill. As he changed gear, his hand accidentally brushed against her. Instinctively she eased herself away from him.

He broke the silence. "Why do you want to see our camp?" he challenged her with suspicion. "Of what interest can it be to you?"

"I want a taste of the real Spain," she answered almost apologetically. "And Paco has offered to teach me the flamenco."

He looked nonplussed. It was not the answer he was expecting. "Well – this is it – the real Spain. There – see over there are the entrances to the caves." He gestured towards them. "However, I do not approve of strangers treating our flamenco frivolously. It is a serious dance for the dedicated."

She grimaced at his now predictable attitude towards her. Her eyes followed his direction with surprise. The white washed entrances were man made, cut deep into the rock face.

"Oh – but I was expecting to see beautiful horse drawn wagons!" she exclaimed.

He looked at her with amusement "Sorry to disappoint you,"

Her bemused expression, made him explain, as if he thought it his duty to enlighten her. "The days of the horse drawn painted wagon are long gone. Some gypsies have replaced them with modern spacious caravans, but our settlement prefers the caves."

This will certainly be a life broadening experience, she thought.

"There is of course one woman who still lives in a painted wagon," went on José. "Infact, when informed of your coming, she insisted you pay her a visit," he added mysteriously.

Starla-sky did not have time to question him further, for a group of exuberant gypsy children, suddenly surrounded the jeep, shouting. "José! Senor José!"

They continued to talk animatedly to him in Spanish, eyeing Starla-sky shyly. Although threadbare their clothes were once carefully embroidered in a flood of bright colours; bare feet and dusky skins, already hardened to the ever shining sun.

A meal was being cooked on a charcoal brazier, the air thick with the smell of coriander and burnt meat. Small children kicked up the dust. Starla-sky felt conspicuously out of place. José jumped down from the jeep and went around opening the door for her. He then called for Paco.

Paco's blonde head could just be seen within a group of raven haired girls, dressed in their traditional finery, Anita amongst them. Men stood in groups alongside.

Paco's face lit up. "Hey – Starla! José took good care of you? I have been preparing the girls to show you the preliminary dance steps."

"Yes," she smiled, never more glad to see a familiar face.

"You are just in time for the meal. Then we shall dance."

People began to gather, circling the brazier. They sat on the ground placidly, while the old women distributed the food. Starla-sky followed Paco, the children giggling around them. She looked around for José, suddenly remembering she really ought to thank him. He was nowhere to be seen.

There was no time to dwell on her guilt. A plate of meat and strange looking vegetables was thrust into her hand, by a toothless aged crone. The woman smiled broadly, gesturing for Starla-sky to eat. Starla-sky thanked her. They all seemed to be awaiting her reaction – all eyes watching.

Gingerly, she picked up the spicy vegetable with her fingers and took a bite. It was certainly different. She managed to swallow, and then smiled, nodding approval. Sounds of appreciation and cheer went around the circle. Everyone started eating and talking.

"They like you," said Paco. "It's a good job you didn't pull a face when you ate."

"They probably would have chased me out of the hills," she laughed. "Anyway, I quite liked the food. Though I hardly eat meat and found it a bit tough."

"Don't let Ana the cook, hear you say that, or she might put the evil eye on you."

Starla-sky shuddered. "She wouldn't – would she?"

"Well, you know our reputation for putting curses and spells on people," he said with tongue in cheek.

"What – and stealing children and drinking their blood," she laughed in devilment.

Ana started to sing in a low melodious voice. When they had all finished eating, they all joined in the song. Wine began to flow and men began to dance. Every now and then, they stopped to pick a partner. Those that were not dancing were playing guitars.

"We are starting early today," Paco informed her. "Usually it is towards dawn, after a nights drinking. The best flamenco is never rehearsed, it erupts spontaneously."

Starla-sky watched the river of movement.

Paco called to Anita. "Take Starla into my cave and give her one of my Mother's flamenco dresses to wear"

"In here," beckoned Anita. "Si - come."

She followed Anita into the cave. It was pleasantly cool and furnished with surprising luxury. Caskets and jars of Byzantine influence were placed on the cupboards. Metal work in bronze, silver, gold and cloisonné wear decorated a large dark wood table.

"Paco keeps his Mother's dresses in this closet." Anita opened a heavy wooden door, to reveal a line of jewel coloured frills spilling out." She smiled at her new friend. "Take your pick. They should be about your size."

Starla-sky's eyes widened. "They are beautiful. I'm spoilt for choice."

"I think the burgundy one is right for you," said Anita, her delicate face glowing.

"Where is Paco's Mother?" asked Starla-sky, puzzled.

"She does not live at the camp." The younger girl's expression suddenly changed. She looked solemn.

Starla-sky lifted the dress up against her. She loved the fine burgundy fitted bodice, the deep frills flaring red and orange below her hips, dipping at the back and rising to her thighs at the front. "I appreciate Paco's kindness."

"Si," agreed Anita.

The dress fitted Starla-sky perfectly. She emerged from the cave to be greeted by sounds of admiration. The women gathered around her, fingering her silken blonde hair.

"Come! Come!" commanded Paco. "Leave her. Now we begin. I will teach you how I was taught by José. True flamenco began from the cante jondo – profound deep song. It extends beyond the known rhythms of any words or music – awakened from the abyss of the soul. A living spirit – creative force."

He described it beautifully, she thought. She could not reconcile these words with José Velázquez, the man who had spoken to her so derisively as if to amuse the black stone of his heart.

This prompted her to ask incredulously. "José taught you this!?

"Si, I owe him a lot. He is older and wiser than me," replied Paco with reverence.

"But he can be so insulting," she considered with annoyance the way he had patronized her.

"Ah, that is because he likes you," was Paco's surprising answer.

Starla-sky gave a short laugh. "Are you kidding me? He has a funny way of showing it."

Paco shook his head. "You don't understand. That is his way of communicating. Usually he would be indifferent."

"He can be that too," she countered tersely recalling how silent he had been.

"He is a proud man who also has a soft heart. He would die for his people."

He must have hidden depths she wasn't aware of, she thought, and said with a hint of cynicism, "What's so special about him?"

"He is a man of great honour and commands our respect." Paco straightened as if to salute. "He is our leader."

Starla-sky mulled this over. "What – you mean like a gypsy king?"

"Si!" Paco shrugged.

She was thoughtful for a moment. "King of the gypsies," she savoured the words slowly. Her interest raised, she had the fleeting impression of being transported to another era.

"Si – look, no more talk." Paco indicated impatiently to the feet of the dancers. "Watch the steps – concentrate."

Painstakingly, he took her through the preliminary movements. An hour later she had mastered enough knowledge to dance the basic steps.

"I think that is enough for your beginner's lesson," said Paco. "My dancers are eager to let the music take them."

A violinist joined the guitarists, blending harmoniously. The lucid strains rose to the quickening of the dancers feet. She watched the riot of colour whirling like Catherine wheels in the moonlight, spellbound. The girls wore flowers in their hair – their ethnic earrings twinkling. Intense emotion set their features. Echoes of handclapping grew louder with cries and shouts.

The old women told Starla-sky it would continue till half-light, before dawn. Though late, the land was still well lit by the moon. As the dancers formed a circle, Starla-sky left to change out of the dress. She decided to slip away and explore.

Lost in thought, she wandered away from the caves and climbed some low rocky hills, overgrown with broom, cistus and lavender. The aroma drifted pleasantly over her. Past a river, she came to a modest village, centred by quite a small town. Unpretentious buildings were surrounded by a shaded wood of pines.

Music drifted out from a Taverna. Obscure dialects could be heard. She was unsure whether to venture any nearer. She decided it would be wise to keep to the outskirts near the pine trees. She had just sat down on a log to rest, when a beggar woman came ambling out of the forest.

Turning her head to one side, she surveyed Starla-sky inquisitively. Her face broke into a gold toothed grin. "Hija de Dios! Hija de Dios!" she wailed excitedly, offering her begging bowl.

Realising she had no money on her, Starla-sky shook her head and got up to walk away.

Venturing a little closer to the town, she could still hear the old beggar woman shrieking behind her. A group of peasant women loitering along the street, turned to see what was going on. Their eyes fixed steadily upon Starla-sky. They were talking loudly amongst themselves now. As she passed by she was aware of the sickly smell of cheap perfume. Their hostility was becoming increasingly obvious.

They started to taunt her. "Ingles? Americano? Beetch!" they hissed.

In her panic, Starla-sky tripped on the uneven ground, just stopping herself from landing on the hard stone. Sounds of raucous laughter exploded in her ears. Two of the women stepped out, blocking her way. She tilted her chin defiantly.

"Let me by," she ordered, desperately masking her fear.

Another woman came up behind her and began unwinding Starla-sky's plait, tugging at her hair. Starla-sky struggled to free herself.

"Parar! Parar!" Suddenly a man's voice roared with authority.

She turned to see José Velázquez marching over towards them. His face looked thunderous. He glowered at the women, shouting at them in Spanish.

Immediately, the woman let go of Starla-sky's hair and nodded gravely at José. The others backed off sheepishly, looking at him in admiration and respect. Roughly, he grabbed Starla-sky by the arm, forcing her away from the scene.

"What in hells name do you think you are doing out alone at this time of night?" he bellowed.

Starla-sky was visibly shaken. "I – I was just taking a walk in the cool evening air."

He took a deep breath, as if it was beyond his comprehension. "These hills are full of banditos. You must be either stupid or naïve."

"Surely one can take an evening stroll?" she argued.

He raised his eyes heavenward. "Madre de Dios! Madre de Dios! Not alone. If you must walk I will accompany you."

"There's no need," she answered curtly. Her hair had fallen loose. She shook it out and ran her fingers through.

Ignoring her snub, he continued. "We can walk back this way and I can enlighten you on what could happen to you – if you remain ignorant to the unsavoury side of our country."

"I don't need you to explain," she retorted, her spark of defiance returning. How dare he try and intimidate her. "I'm sure I could have dealt with a few high spirited peasant women."

"Peasant women?" he snapped. "Peasant women they may be. Do not be so foolish Starla-sky. Those peasant women are whores of the hills. Shocked? Don't be, this is a poor country. They live in the poorer villages"

She did indeed look genuinely shocked.

"They know I disapprove," he said arrogantly. "They will not approach me."

"Why would they want to attack me?"

"They thought you were invading their pitch," he said matter of factly. "No decent woman would be out alone this late."

"What? How degrading." She was appalled at their presumption of her.

"Who are you to judge them? You know nothing of their wretched lives."

"I would not presume to do so."

He cast his eyes over her smooth, delicate skin. Her cheeks flushed beneath the bloom of her recently acquired golden tan.

Cupping her chin in his hand, he said. "What do you know of their suffering? You, from – let me guess – a middle class English background? Huh – we gypsies have suffered for centuries!"

She pulled away. Maybe not with the hardships they had endured, but emotionally – yes. Some suffering did not show on the surface. There was no physical presence. It was only if one was sensitive enough to notice the sadness in the eyes, hidden beneath the rebellious front.

"This country has double standards. On the one hand the men demand their women to be virtuous and on the other…" She indicated back towards the village. "This goes on."

"Do not talk about something you know nothing about," he said with a disarming coldness.

"Who said I know nothing about it," she replied, attempting to sound worldly.

"Ah – perhaps you are familiar with the profession, quiredo?"

"I am not ignorant!"

His eyes narrowed. "Tell me about it?"

"Surely you don't need me to tell you," she retorted, determined not to bow to intimidation.

"You like the men?" he asked, looking at her strangely.

"I like men, yes. Why shouldn't I?" She started to walk on ahead.

"Indeed, why not?" He said as he caught up with her.

"They can be good company. I have many friends of both sexes," she replied with sincerity and wished at this moment she was back on familiar ground, socialising down at her local pub.

"And they show you a good time?" He added, not letting the subject drop.

"We can all enjoy ourselves – men and women." She wished he would stop this line of conversation, only too aware that their thoughts crossed cultures.

He digested this for a moment, and then said pointedly. "I do not want your influence to corrupt my sister Anita."

"What?" she spluttered. "I can assure you I have no intention…"

He interrupted her. "Anita imitates you – she wants to look like you and your kind, and stay out late at the disco. She will listen to no one."

They had come to the other side of the forest. The trees cast shadows across his features, playing ghostly tricks. Between the branches Starla-sky could see the shifty face of the mountains beyond. Jose glared at her with treacherous pool-deep eyes.

"I know how it is in your country, changing boyfriends every other week. Is that how it is with you querido?"

"That's none of your business," she shook with anger.

"Ah - so it is true." He was standing over her menacingly.

He bent his head closer and took hold of her shoulders. The heat of his hands made her weak. Was he about to kiss her? She closed her eyes and clenched her fists. They were alone in the forest. He could do whatever he wanted. She waited expectantly. He looked at her with fire in his eyes. Her breath quickened.

"You have a lot to learn. Our ways are far removed from what you are used to." His face darkened. "If you are to remain safe whilst here in the caves, you must behave as our women do?"

He let go of her. His fingers probing her skin, coercing her into submission, had ignited dormant emotions. She wondered how those same fingers would feel if he had love in his heart. He had excited her. There was a fine line between love and hate, she construed.

The dancing was still in full swing when they reached the camp. Discreetly, she slipped back in amongst the old women and children, dozing in the dark. It appeared no one had noticed her absence. The day had exhausted her. Eventually, she lay back on the earth, closed her eyes and drifted off with the sounds of the night.

Much later, she was vaguely aware of two strong arms gently lifting her up and carrying her into the cave.

She awoke the next morning to the smell of cooking and smoke from the brazier. She was still clothed. Anita stirred beside her in the oversize bed.

"Oh – good morning Anita," she said in surprise.

Anita opened her eyes and blinked. "Hi Starla-sky," she said stretching her arms above her head. "I hope you don't mind sharing with me. José was concerned about you. He tried not to wake you last night when he carried you in." She rolled over onto her stomach and rested her hands under her chin. "He has a soft spot for you."

"Really?" replied Starla-sky in disbelief, dismissing the ludicrous notion.

"You had better get up," announced Anita. "Paco has arranged a visit with the wise woman. You've got half an hour."

Chapter 5

Halfway up the mountain slope, Starla-sky stopped to catch her breath. "How much further Paco?" she panted. "Who is this woman who lives like a hermit?"

"Her name is Rosario," he answered, then added. "She is my Grandmother."

Starla-sky wiped her hand across her brow. A charming brightly painted wagon could just be seen at the top of the hill, half hidden by a canopy of protruding rock; which did a good job of shading it from the rays of sun. They approached reverently, out of respect for the occupant. But they needn't have bothered, for she had been aware of them before their feet had taken the first step on the path.

Rosario was sitting beneath an ancient fig tree. A small woman – her wizened nut brown face etched with wrinkles; white hair billowing about her shoulders. Her black eyes fastened on Starla-sky.

"Come closer Niña," she said in a throaty voice.

Paco pushed Starla-sky forward.

"Si – now I see her." Rosario looked from one to the other. "Paco's Father was my son – Pablo Herrera," she informed Starla-sky. "He has gone from here." She touched the earth with outstretched fingers. "But not from here," she laid a hand on her heart, and then raised her arms heavenward. "Beyond the stars – gone but not forgotten."

Starla-sky stood transfixed. She wasn't sure how to react. "Thank you for inviting me," she said in the spellbound silence. "You speak good English."

"Ah – an angel taught me," replied Rosario mysteriously. She then turned to Paco and spoke in Spanish.

"Si! Si!" Paco smiled.

"What did she say," whispered Starla-sky.

Rosario was grinning from ear to ear. She began to hum softly.

"She says you come from some strange land, beyond the moon," whispered Paco. "You bring with you the light from the star of the west. She says you shall unite with the light from the star of the east."

Rosario raised her head. "I foresee a night of joyous dancing – dancing till the moon goes down."

"I don't understand," said Starla-sky.

"The night of full moon," murmured Rosario. "Shush! Spirit of tree is talking. Can you not feel its presence?"

Starla-sky silently tuned in to the energy.

Quick as lightening Rosario stepped up into her caravan. "Come - Niña," she beckoned.

Starla-sky followed, entering a spotless interior, cluttered throughout with brass ornaments, embroidered cushions and shawls. A black silk scarf covered a round object in the middle of the table. Rosario motioned for her to sit. She lifted the scarf and prism- split lights danced about the room, from a dazzling crystal sphere.

Starla-sky blinked as the old woman gazed placidly into the centre.

Eventually, Rosario spoke. "I see ancient wall." She appeared to be seeing a vision.

Starla-sky suspected she was seeing hallucinatory pictures. "A wall?" she asked, with some scepticism.

Rosario continued. "Someone has difficulty dismantling wall."

Starla-sky looked baffled.

"This - symbolic. Talks of unhappiness in your past. You felt disillusionment - rejection – Si?"

Starla-sky nodded in agreement.

"But all this is passing. You must not dig in hall of memories. After storm comes calm – after rain comes sunshine. But first there is barrier to be pulled down between two persons." She raised her head from the crystal ball and looked Starla-sky straight in the eye. "Beauty is gift. Do not misuse it. Be discriminating. For you have test of fire and temptation to go through yet – comprende?"

Starla-sky wondered with alarm what she meant.

"You inherited gift of clairaudience. Once aware of this all will become clear. You have dealt with harsh Karma in this life time. Your heart over shadowed, blocking the way from those who would help you in spirit. Let go futile fears, Niña. Break the bonds – be true to inner light. Turn face towards sun. You look but you do not truly see."

Starla-sky was conscious of an uncomfortable sensation. "You seem to know a lot about me," she ventured warily.

Rosario peered back into the crystal and murmured. "Within inner silence there are powerful forces to be harnessed. I see you have lot of love to give."

"How will I know if I am on the right path?"

Rosario raised her eyes. "Why you think you have come here Niña? We have been waiting for you. For work of spirit to be successful, polarities have to be balanced. Nothing happens by chance. If you fight destiny, illness and inharmony will follow. You must obey almighty power we are all part of."

"But – what is my destiny?"

"We have been granted free will. Follow inner conscience. Seek inner stillness of pure spirit. In this shall lay your strength. It is simple as that."

"I know," said Starla-sky. Now why had she said that? For a split second the knowledge had flashed into her mind.

"There are many questions inside you. Your thoughts confused - in turmoil," said Rosario.

Unexpected tears sprang up behind Starla-sky's eyes. "Who am I, Rosario?" she pleaded.

"When ready you find answer in the Patio de los Leones. It is not for me to tell you. I cannot interfere with your Karma. Now go - experience life – be happy. Bless you Niña."

Starla-sky's instinct was to jump up and hug Rosario, but an unfamiliar reserve held her back. She opened the wagon door. "Thank you Rosario," she whispered.

The old woman smiled. "Tell Paco - enter."

Starla-sky sat on the grassy slope waiting for Paco to reappear and mulled over the wise woman's words. She had given her much to think about.

Half an hour later they headed back down the path. Paco was unusually quiet, not his talkative self. Starla-sky was inquisitive as to what Rosario had said to him. She felt it unwise to pry into his deep thoughts, and fell silent, lost in her own.

Strangely, not a single word was uttered between them about it. Her thoughts turned to José. She wanted to know how confined the gypsy women were.

She broke the silence. "Paco – do the women ever go to the village? I understand they are not allowed there in the evening."

"That is so. It is unsafe territory at night."

"José goes there."

"Yes he went to Granada to discuss the festival of music and dance, with the great Antonio el Garcia Martinez. He is the teacher of flamenco in Granada." By his tone, Paco obviously held the man in high esteem. "And on the journey home, José usually stops off at the Taverna in village de Carlos."

"What is this festival?"

"It is very exciting annual event," replied Paco, and then added proudly. "And we – José Velázquez dancers are important participants."

Starla-sky's interest was raised. "It sounds great."

"Si – it's held next month. If you practise hard enough, you may be allowed to be included in the dance."

Her eyes lit up. "Wow – do you think so? Will I have a partner?" She wondered idly how it would be to dance with José. Then she remembered Marcia and said. "I haven't seen Marcia at the camp."

"There are plenty who will be willing to partner you. And – no, you won't see Marcia. She only accompanies José when we dance for tourists or parties. Otherwise she remains in Granada. Occasionally she will grace us with her presence at the camp for a celebration."

"Marcia lives in Granada?"

"Si – she is the daughter of Antonio el Garcia Martinez."

Oh – of course." She suddenly recalled. "I've heard of her. Isn't she the famous flamenco dancer Marcia Martinez?"

"The very same! It is expected she and José will marry."

Starla-sky gulped. "What? Oh – when?"

"Soon, I expect if Marcia has her way. She has made it known she wants José to go and live with her in the comfort of Granada. However, it is against his principles. I'm sure if he cannot persuade her to come and live at the camp, the whole affair is doomed." Paco shrugged. "But who knows, José's charm can be persuasive."

This was indeed unexpected news to Starla-sky. She wondered how Anita would feel if José left the caves.

As soon as they arrived back Anita was waiting to hear her news.

"Rosario is an interesting woman. She has much wisdom," Starla-sky told her, and then added. "Anita, would you ever go back to America?"

"No - never. I would be too homesick."

"Don't you miss your parents?"

"Sure I do. But my heart is here. My parents are good people. They are doing good work in America for the travelling community. It is right for them, but it is not my Karma."

"You believe in Karma?"

"Of course. Don't you?"

"Well – I've never given it much thought – but, yes, I suppose I do."

"And what is your Karma then, Starla-sky?" probed Anita.

"That's a difficult one," Starla-sky looked thoughtful. "What about you?"

"That's easy. My mission for this life is to live amongst my people – in the country of my birth – and as I work with them, I shall learn much from them, in order for my soul to progress."

"Have you always been so sure?"

"Si, ever since I was a child."

"You are lucky. I've never really known what I wanted. Or if I did it probably wasn't right for me."

"There was a time when I was uncertain too," confided Anita. "I didn't know which way to turn."

"And how did you solve the problem?"

"Oh – I went to see the wise woman, and she put me back on the right path. She sees all and knows all. She helped me understand the spiritual law of true justice."

"What is true justice – I should like to know?"

"She explained that the experiences of joy or pain we attract to ourselves have been created within us by our past actions. It is a simple matter of cause and effect."

"I can see that. It's so true," Starla-sky had this sudden feeling deep in her soul of just knowing this was feasible." "This I must remember, should I suffer any injustice."

Anita looked at her earnestly. "You may think you have suffered unjustly, but it is what you have earned by disregarding the law of truth which governs all life. I cannot escape and nor can you – or anyone of us."

"I am learning so much this weekend. Anita you have opened my mind. I want to learn so much more."

"Rosario taught me to develop clear vision, for only then can I recognise the unseen forces at work. Now I appreciate the outworking of spiritual law and the setting in which I have been placed."

"I know now nothing happens by chance." Starla-sky sighed, "I just want to forget the negative happenings in my past and find my true path."

"Out of the ashes of the old life shall arise the new life," Anita said sympathetically. "You see, I had to be patient and wait until I was certain in my mind. Now I try always to have faith and put my life in the hands of my creator, the great White Spirit."

Starla-sky put her hand on Anita's arm. "You are so wise – what a beautiful philosophy."

"Did you not know Starla-sky – my family and Paco's family are descendants from an ancient tribe of travelling seers and mystics?"

Wow – how romantic," exclaimed Starla-sky. "There is so much I want to know about this life. Such a shame the weekend is nearly over."

Chapter 6

The drive back to Puerto Banus via Granada was pleasant. Paco was not such an erratic driver as José, preferring to travel at leisure. Starla-sky had come to realise that Paco treated life as a celebration. He did things in his own time, in his easy going manner.

Gently, they made their way past upland plains; fertile crops, alternating with barren hills, deep pools, thickets of trees and vast fields of corn. Andalusia was indeed a land of contrasts, thought Starla-sky, as she looked back over her shoulder, to the peak of the Sierra Mountains, way behind and above her.

Paco followed her gaze. "I suppose you fancy mountain climbing now!" he joked.

"I think I'll pass on that one. That's probably a bit too adventurous for me," she laughed. "I have my limitations – I'm not completely mad."

"No – not completely, but well on the way," he teased.

She grimaced. "Hmm! I also have my weaknesses – and one is heights, I'm afraid."

"In that case you can forget the mountain and stick to flamenco dancing, with your feet well and truly planted on the ground. The highest mountain peak is ten thousand metres," Paco informed her. "Life is precarious in these regions. One thing we can rely on though is the earth supplying us with a constant richness of flowers, fruits and corn. Certain seasons we have an abundant organic supermarket."

Starla-sky laughed. "That's an unusual turn of phrase to describe it – supermarket!"

"Si – you know – natures own supermarket."

"I understand Paco – you put it well. I've come to the conclusion you are as crazy as me!"

He nodded in reluctant agreement.

Most of the valley had been left to grow wild. A few typical Andalusian style houses in cobbled streets could be seen at the top of a hill overlooking a Franciscan monastery.

On again, out of the village, Starla-sky was captivated by the remoteness of the land, fringed by towering forests. It was mid-day before they reached the town of Granada. Time, holding no meaning for Paco, he suggested they stop to eat.

"There's no hurry is there?" he said lazily.

"Not really. That's a good idea. I'm sure my Aunt can wait a little longer to hear about my adventure." She was looking forward to telling her and could just picture Aunt Jessie throwing questions at her excitedly.

Starla-sky felt like a fake foreign tourist. She was reminded of the Moors invading with the fervour of the prophet's message – marching on the road to paradise. She had tasted the life of a nomadic tribe.

After a leisurely lunch they continued east to Puerto Banus and soon Paco was dropping Starla-sky off outside the villa. "I will see you next Friday for your flamenco lesson – Granada – same time. Okay – one of us will meet you. Adios."

"Adios Paco – and thank you," she called after him, and waited until he had gone, before going inside.

The villa held an unusual silence. She glanced around the white walled room, stepping carefully across the honey coloured tiled floor. The excited reception she was half expecting, wasn't to be.

"Aunt Jessie, are you in?" she called softly.

There was no response. Perhaps her Aunt was still at the hotel, it was early yet. Opening the fridge door, just about to take out a cool drink, she heard a muffled sob.

"Starla-sky – is that you dear?" Aunt Jessie sounded distressed.

"Yes." Hurrying into the bedroom, she found her Aunt dabbing her eyes with a handkerchief. "Whatever's wrong Aunt Jessie?"

"It's Federico – he's been threatened," responded Aunt Jessie between sobs.

"Threatened?" It was beyond Starla-sky's belief that anyone would want to harm her Aunts charming husband Federico.

"Some rich villains," replied Aunt Jessie, her voice shaking. "They've bought a vacant plot of land and now find it difficult to get planning permission. They know how prosperous our hotel is and want it for themselves."

"But they can't …" It was preposterous.

"They can. They think they can do whatever they want and God help anyone who stands in their way." Aunt Jessie let out a deep sigh. "They have offered a vast amount in a take over bid and told Federico they will harm his family if he refuses."

"Have you contacted the police?" asked Starla-sky, trying to remain calm.

"No – you don't know what these people are capable of. This isn't called the Costa del Crime for nothing."

"Federico isn't going to give into their demands, is he?"

"No – I'm so afraid."

"Try not to worry Aunt Jessie." Starla-sky felt remarkably level headed under the circumstances. "Where is Federico now?"

"He's at the hotel. He said he would sort this out his own way."

"I'm sure he knows what he's doing."

"I don't know." Aunt Jessie rose to her feet, her usual vigour now replaced by panic. "We must pack what we need and go to the hotel. This villa is too remote."

By the time they arrived at the hotel, Starla-sky had managed to calm her Aunt considerably. Federico hastily ushered them inside.

"You be safe here. I hire two bodyguards – one for inside the hotel and one for Starla-sky if she wishes to go out. I've had talk with José Velázquez and he agree to look after Starla-sky."

"What!" gasped Starla-sky, all her courage plummeting. "I don't need a bodyguard. I will not let these thugs scare me."

"I cannot jeopardise your safety," Federico answered firmly. "I appreciate you are a tower of strength for your Aunt, but you have to be protected."

Starla-sky pressed her lips together firmly. Why did it have to be José Velázquez? Damn thugs! However, she had not come to Spain to be locked in a hotel room. Her Aunt was looking at her in a state of anxiety, about to burst into tears.

"Don't worry, I'll do as you say," relented Starla-sky and squeezed Aunt Jessie's hand. There was no option.

José arrived later that evening. Starla-sky greeted him curtly.

"We must keep this confidential," began José, "Amongst ourselves – it would be foolish to discuss this outside these four walls." He turned his attention to Starla-sky. "Are you listening?"

"Walls have ears," she replied with a hint of sarcasm. His manner was already annoying her.

He glared at her. "I hope you are taking this seriously – do you realise your life is at risk?"

"Okay, I know," Starla-sky snapped irritably. However was she going to survive the ordeal of spending so much time with this arrogant man?

Aunt Jessie looked from one to the other. "I think we've all had a hard day. Let's get some sleep."

"You're right, let us sleep on it" agreed José with an air of authority "Perhaps some of us will be in a more pleasant mood tomorrow." He stood up to his full height. "Which is my room Federico?"

He wasn't staying here, was he? For a moment Starla-sky thought she was going to have a panic attack.

"I will show you José. It is the smallest room." Federico waived a hand in apology.

José took a step towards the door. He turned and nodded at Starla-sky. His expression held concealed amusement. It struck her how powerful he looked.

She wondered who she had to fear the most, José Velázquez or the villains.

She went to her room and locked the door. Sheer mental exhaustion prevented her from sleeping. She lay awake only too conscious of José's presence next door. He was probably sleeping like a baby, she grimaced.

She started to drift in and out of sleep. Her mind was full of the eventful weekend; Paco, the flamenco dancers, Anita and the words of the wise woman. She pondered over her encounter with José in the village. Had he almost kissed her in the forest? The memory made her tingle. Did some primitive desire wish he had? What urge lying dormant within her had risen to the surface? The hot climate was certainly doing strange things to her.

He thought her just another brazen tourist, she suspected. After all he was planning to marry the virtuous Marcia – who would, no doubt, slot neatly into place, on the doormat of his ego. No- more to the point – what did she think of him? As she eventually fell asleep her jumbled thoughts were a mixture of anger and confusion.

"Croissants and coffee?" José cocked his head to one side and raised an eyebrow.

Starla-sky crossed the room purposefully. She had hoped to be up before him, to eat her breakfast alone. "Where's my Aunt and Federico?" she demanded coolly, ignoring his question.

"They arose early." He began to pour coffee into his mug with his back to her. "They are downstairs already, working."

Wrenching her eyes away from the broadness of his shoulders, she said quickly "I better go and see if they need any help."

"No you don't." He swung round. His glance swept over her freshly combed hair, tumbling down her back, and the white top and shorts. "There's no point – and you are not dressed for working. Starlasky, do you want any croissants or not?"

"I never eat breakfast," she lied, and then snapped. "And please don't tell me what not to do."

His face hardened and he struck a commanding hand on the table, causing her to jump. "For your own safety, just do as I tell you - and," he emphasized, "you should eat something."

"Why should I eat just because you say so?" she retorted, aware she was being factitious.

"I can see you are going to be difficult," he drawled, taking a sip of his coffee.

"Difficult!" she almost shrieked. "I'm a grown woman, not a child." She pushed her hair away from her face and raised her chin. This arrangement was not going to work. She would have to talk to Federico.

"Well, it's undeniable you are a woman, but…" he flicked his eyes over her and shrugged sardonically.

She gritted her teeth. "I suppose that's all that is obvious to you in a woman – her body!" Too late she regretted her impulsive tongue.

"Far from it. What's a body without a mind?" He spoke quietly with an edge of controlled anger.

Some mischievous spirit inside her spurred her on to test his limitations. "I should think a simple servile woman with a good childbearing body would suit you," she suggested boldly.

"You would, would you?" His mouth twisted with amusement. "Perhaps you're right. Then again, you're an expert on men – eh querido?"

"What?" She would like to have wiped the impudent smile from his face. Instead she said evenly. "I have a certain experience of your type – yes."

"Ah." He raised an inquiring eyebrow. "Type? That's narrowed things down – usually spoken from the lips of a spurned woman."

"No – a realistic woman," she countered, looking him straight in the eye. Why did he have to hold such biased opinions? Was he humouring her?

"I am familiar with the saying – hell hath no fury like a woman scorned – comprende?" he informed her.

She wasn't going to continue with this line of conversation. "How will your fiancé feel about you spending all this time with me?" she asked, changing the subject.

"I am not beholden to any woman," he replied.

"Don't let Marcia hear you say that," she reminded him.

"Marcia?" he said sharply. "I am not answerable to Marcia."

Starla-sky detected his face darken. His shocked surprise led her to believe he had wanted to keep this information from her.

"That's not what I heard."

He took an intake of breath. His features set, revealing nothing. "You should not believe all you hear."

"Really?" She caught his eye for a second.

The muscles in his cheeks tightened. "That's enough. It is none of your business. I forbid you to talk on the subject again."

"Forbid?" she looked at him defiantly, her eyes widening.

The expression on his face told her she had probed too deep. But, to forbid her? Who did he think he was? First he had ordered her not to visit the Village de Carlos. On that occasion she had not come across any banditos, as he had suggested! Now it seemed he was forbidding her to venture out without him. She would not be held prisoner!

"So my conversation is to be vetted now?" she grumbled. Her hair fell forward across her face as she gripped the chair, irately.

"Don't push your luck Starla-sky," he growled, holding her gaze steadily. "Look – seeing as we have been forced together – and I dislike it as much as you do – I think for the sake of sanity we should try to be a little more civil towards each other – don't you?"

Starla-sky shrugged. She lifted her hair, flung it back over her shoulder and attempted to match his stony expression.

Jose appeared unnerved. "I am taking this job on for the soul purpose of helping my amigo Federico. The last thing I want is to impose myself on a girl who, so obviously, despises me."

"It is not in my nature to despise anyone," she retorted.

He ignored her remark and continued. "I assured Federico he can rely on me. I intend to carry out my assignment to the best of my ability. And that means you must put your trust in me at all times – comprende?"

Starla-sky scowled petulantly. "I suppose so." She intended doing as she always did – listen, and then do as she pleased.

She had learned these tactics in her childhood. Aunt Eleanor had tried to suppress her individuality. She smiled at the memory of the horrified expression on Aunt Eleanor's face, when once Starla-sky had arrived home with a bright pink Mohican hairdo. She very cleverly excused herself by convincing her aunt, that it was the shops policy to experiment on the staff.

"That's better." José sat back in his chair and handed her the plate of croissants. "Now how about making a start with these?"

She sat down, raised her eyes and caught his. For all her bravado, she felt trapped. Grudgingly, she took the croissant. She would play the game. For that was all it was, or at least she would make it so. She mulled it over in her head and came to a solution. In order to survive this unfortunate episode, she decided to turn it into a competition. She had the upper hand; especially as he was unaware he was competing. He couldn't win. It would be a challenge.

She surmised, so far, he had proceeded to antagonise her with his flagrant rudeness. She would be more subtle. Her hidden reserves of strength were a power she could call on in times of emergency.

She took a bite of the croissant and studied him closely. His face showed no sign of weakness. To win the first round would take all her self control. If she so much as lost her cool once, he would notch up the first point. The challenge was thrilling and she was confident he would soon be eating out of her hand.

"I think I'll have that coffee now please," she said agreeably.

"Bravo!" There was no surprise in his voice. He was used to people coming round to his way of thinking. "Buento Senorita," he smiled.

"Gracias," she accepted the cup gratefully, but the smile that curved her mouth didn't quite reach her eyes. One point to me, she thought, patronizing chauvinist that he is!

"This morning we stay here," he stated, relieved at her now reasonable attitude. "I realise it would be unfair to keep you indoors all day, so – I will take you to the beach after lunch. There will be no wandering off alone – got it?"

She flinched, he was doing it again – giving out orders and she expected, enjoying it. His overbearing attitude didn't make it any the easier. Luckily for him, the smooth taste of the coffee had a rejuvenating effect on her.

"Whatever you say," she adopted the fixed smile again, and was tempted to add, 'my master.'

He continued. "We will not stick to a routine. If these people are watching out for us, as I'm sure they are, that may prove dangerous. Any suggestions?"

She blinked with surprise. He wasn't actually asking her advice, was he? For a moment it threw her. She was not expected to be allowed to hold an opinion. This was her chance to soar ahead in the points score. Quite amicably she would lay down some rules of her own.

"Firstly, I suggest we help out in the hotel. No one would dare try anything amongst the guests." At least she would not be cooped up alone in here with him. "And secondly, I need my privacy. When I want to read or write a letter, I shall retreat to my room – alone."

"Well – I guess…" he began.

"Also," she cut in. "I plan to meet Paco in Granada on Friday for my flamenco lesson. Any objections?"

"No", he answered without hesitation. She thought he was showing amazing self restraint. "No," he repeated. "I shall be the one to take you. Infact querido that is the most sensible suggestion you have made yet."

"Oh – why?" she asked apprehensively.

"Can't you see? I should have thought of that. The gypsy caves will be the ideal hiding place. These Ingles villains have no knowledge of these parts."

She smiled wryly. They had both scored a point equally.

By the time the waiter arrived with their lunch, Starla-sky was pacing the room like a caged animal.

Restlessly, she walked over to the window and pulled the blind.

"No!" Jose bellowed.

She turned sharply to face him. "For God sake – what have I done now?"

"It will be in your best interests to keep away from the window," he said evenly, aware of her nervous unease.

"Okay – there's no need to overreact." She gritted her teeth. Don't lose control, she reminded herself. One point to him!

"Come and eat lunch, then we can get out of here and go to the beach. I know this is trying for you – but we can beat it together."

No, not together, she thought. I can do this alone, as you'll soon find out. Once she was with Paco in the freedom of the hills she would not need José.

Chapter 7

José stopped the jeep as near to the beach at Puerto Banus as possible. Once away from the confines of the hotel room, Starla-sky began to relax. Boats on the marina vied for attention with trendy boutiques. Starla-sky flicked through a rail of brightly coloured swimwear outside a shop. A red bikini caught her eye.

"You want?" asked José.

"No – I have brought one with me."

"But, you like the red one." It was a statement, more than a question.

"Yes – but…" she shrugged

"In that case I will buy it for you."

"No," she protested. "I have money of my own if I wish to purchase it."

"I do not approve of such a garment," he said dubiously, "but, as I will be accompanying you at all times, I guess you can't get into too much trouble."

"What!" she exclaimed. "Have you been to the beach lately? Do you know what girls are wearing?"

"Of course."

"Then you must know – it's not much more than a thong, and sometimes even less."

"My people hold women as precious jewels. They have to be protected and dress modestly"

Her eyes widened. She thought it highly romantic, but archaic. "What century are you living in?"

He had already turned on his heels impatiently, grabbed the red bikini and was paying for it.

"What are you doing? I haven't tried it on," she protested.

The saleswoman pointed to the changing cubicle, and smiling expectantly, handed Starla-sky the red bikini. There was nothing she could do, but comply. Slipping it on she found it fitted exquisitely, like a second skin over her curves.

"Senorita – ees right fit?" called the saleswoman.

"Si, perfect," answered Starla-sky.

The woman poked her head around the curtain. "Show – el novia – eh boyfriend?" she urged with typical Spanish enthusiasm.

"He's not…" began Starla-sky.

"Come out and let me see if I approve," interrupted José. The humour in his voice as he played along with the fiasco infuriated her.

The saleswoman nodded to him. "Hermosa! Beautiful Senorita." She pulled back the curtain, forcing Starla-sky to step out.

The way Jose was looking at her made her feel overexposed.

"Si! Si! Querido," he gasped.

"Cut it out," she hissed, when she got close enough for him to hear and out of earshot of the saleswoman. He was obviously overdoing the boyfriend bit.

"You might as well keep it on. We are practically on the beach," he said sliding an arm around her waist.

The saleswoman sighed. "Enjoy your swim."

"Gracias – we will," José winked at her with amusement.

He was revelling in this, thought Starla-sky angrily. "It isn't funny José. I am not your girlfriend."

"That's as maybe. However it has given me an idea. There may come a time when you will have to pretend to be."

"What do you mean?" Alarm bells sounded in her ears.

"Trust me," he assured her. "They will be looking for Federico's niece not a pair of lovers."

Surely he was joking, she thought. She was forever baffled by the workings of his mind. However, he wasn't laughing.

Not wanting to listen to anymore of his reckless ideas, she ran on ahead. "I'm going for a swim," she called back over her shoulder.

The water was inviting. The temperature was cooling. She responded shamelessly to the rippling waves, gently caressing her skin. Under the surface, she dived, and emerged to see José stripping off his jeans and tee shirt. He came towards her dressed in navy trunks. She drank in the sight of his steel hard muscular body – the body of a well trained dancer – toned to perfection. Starla-sky quickly looked away, endeavouring to escape the tremulous feelings he was evoking.

He reached the water and without hesitating, dived straight in. Circling her, he invited her to follow him to a group of high rocks. He was a strong swimmer and was way ahead of her.

Stretching out to the rocky cleft, he pulled himself up. Starla-sky glided towards him. He held his hand out to help her up. His firm touch made her tingle. Hastily she withdrew her hand and sat beside him. His face softened as he looked out over the bay, sheltered by the Sierra Blanca Mountains.

"The enchanting mountains of Spain," he murmured possessively.

"Glorious," she said softly, breathing in the salty smell of the sea.

"Everything we need is here – the earth, the trees, the birds, the sun and stars and moon at night. In my mountains the world is bountiful – a thing of wonder – and all created for mankind. We are custodians of this land" In his thoughts he was back in his own territory – the caves.

Starla-sky was aware that his face exuded an inner light. He was capable of arousing deep profound emotions within her when he spoke like this. Could she compete with his strength of character? Was she strong enough to win the game? Perhaps the real fight was just beginning. Desperately she fought for words to defuse the situation. "Tell me about your mountains," she urged gently.

He dragged his eyes away and looked at her as if he had only become aware of her presence. "All of Spain querido is a constellation of mountains and streams with shallow coastal plains - Andalusia," he savoured the word with deep felt knowledge. "Poets called it paradise on earth, refreshed by sweet waters."

Starla-sky gazed pensively down at the sea; a transparent vast mirror absorbing their faces in the glittering sunlight – merging their reflections together. For that single moment in time they had fused together in the water and become as one. She was mesmerized.

Sudden ripples from a passing peddle boat, shattered her illusions, distorting their features. José stood up and dived back in, leaving Starla-sky's broken image in the water like a jilted bride. As if to banish some irrational omen, she quickly dived in and away from her own solitary reflection.

Nonchantly, José strolled up the beach, across the sand. All eyes turning in his direction from bikini clad girls did not go unnoticed by Starla-sky. A surge of pride made her catch up with him rapidly. She was tempted to link her arm through his in a grand show of possession but checked herself in time. It must be the heat affecting her…

Late afternoon José suggested they should make their way back to the hotel. "We can stop to refresh ourselves with some gazpacho in the Square of the Orange Trees," he suggested.

Starla-sky stirred in the sun. She didn't want to be brought back to reality. "I was almost asleep."

"All the more reason we should go." José appraised her glistening body. He stroked his fingers along her arm. "You're very hot querido," he murmured huskily. "You'll end up with sunstroke."

"Nonsense!" She got up and reached for her shorts, suddenly in a desperate hurry to go.

José grabbed her hand and propelled her towards the jeep. The afternoon at the beach had relaxed them considerably. The swim had absolved Starla-sky's frustration. She had to admit José had been good company.

"Feel better querido?" José inquired as they turned into the main street. "I have a remedy for sunburn given to me by Rosario. I shall apply it to your skin later."

"It's not that bad," she replied hastily.

"I insist. You are my responsibility." His face was stern and Starla-sky had the sense of being overpowered. How would she get out of this?

The Square of the Orange Trees with its white tables and chairs was busy. A day on the beach was often followed by refreshments in the square.

José led Starla-sky to a table for two in the centre, amidst the throng. "We should be inconspicuous here," he informed her.

"Yes – of course." She had almost forgotten the unsavoury business back at the hotel. Furtively she glanced over her shoulder. A shady trellis of vines began above the door in the corner, extending over the patio. A flautist was standing outside, the notes trickling merrily like birdsong. A waiter approached them immediately and José ordered the iced soup.

"I must admit its pleasant here," remarked Starla-sky.

"I guess the atmosphere has recharged your batteries."

"Could be," she reflected. "What about you?"

"What about me?" He asked evasively.

"Well – does it do something for you?"

"It depends…" He held her eyes across the table taunting her. "It depends who I am with."

She pulled a wry face. It was a straightforward question but he seemed to be going off on a tangent.

He looked down at his hands and became serious. "It's all very agreeable but I'm adverse to all this."

"All what?" She was becoming accustomed to these opinionated sides to his character.

"Mass tourism," he gestured around him, "the whole of the Costa del Sol…"

"Doesn't it bring prosperity though?"

"It's gone too far. It's destroyed the structure of society – an entire way of life. Whole villages have disappeared."

"I know what you mean."

"Do you?" He raised an eyebrow. "Do you really Starla-sky? I think not." He looked disdainfully around. "All I see is a foreign settlement – a concrete jungle!"

"And you see me as the foreigner – is that it Jose?"

"That's an unfair question," he replied.

"Is it?" she murmured quietly under her breath, then let the subject drop. As much as she would liked to have argued with him, deep down she knew it would unleash feelings in him which perhaps, she could not handle.

Their attention was diverted by the flute player as he passed by their table. He stopped nearby continuing a bright melody, clear as fountain water.

"I love the spontaneity of the musicians and dancers in Spain," enthused Starla-sky. "It makes life so vibrant."

"We like to live life to the full - sensual delight," replied Jose. "Talking of which – how about a churro and coffee? They do the most delicious doughnuts – pure sensual delight."

"Mmm! You've talked me into it," breathed Starla-sky, her eyes half closed in anticipation.

"I wonder what else you could be talked into?" murmured José provocatively, a smile playing at the corner of his mouth.

Starla-sky's eyes widened. "Nothing I didn't want to, I can assure you!"

"I believe you," he mused.

She raised her chin. "I can be tough when needed."

"I am sure you can querido."

"I know my own mind."

"Si," he acknowledged. "And I'm sure whatever Starla-sky wants, Starla-sky gets."

"Of course," she quipped flippantly. He was beginning to annoy her.

"At any cost?" he asked, one brow raised.

"What do you think? You seem to think you know me."

José lay back in his chair, eyeing her shrewdly. "You've got it all haven't you, beauty and brains? No doubt you use your looks to your advantage, but your brains….?"

"What about my brains?" she snapped defensively.

"Perhaps you haven't learnt to use them yet with common sense – and compassion."

For a moment Starla-sky was speechless. She glared at him, tight lipped. His steady gaze unnerved her.

José continued. "How old are you querido?"

"Twenty three," she said through gritted teeth.

"Ah, twenty three," he repeated, appraising her fresh face, devoid of makeup. "You look so innocent. However, appearances can be deceptive. My guess is you have come far from sweet sixteen and never been kissed."

Starla-sky was livid. "Yes that's right. I use men before they can use me!" He most definitely asked for that answer, she thought angrily.

"And what makes you think men want to treat you like that?"

"All men are the same. If given the chance they take their pleasure and then drop you." The words spilled from her mouth before she had activated her brain. Deep down she knew it wasn't true. Oh God one point to him. She wanted to win.

He leaned forward, his face serious "And you – do you take your pleasure too?"

"Of course!"

His face darkened. "I have been testing you querido. I was willing to give you the benefit of doubt. I suppose many lovers have enjoyed your charms."

"Maybe, I don't recall," she shrugged. Why was he provoking her to say these things?

"I would have thought something as special as making love, you would remember?" he looked outraged.

"What is so special about it?" She wanted to shock him – tear apart his complacency – his self opinionated slander of her character. "I've lost count," she threw the words out carelessly.

The shocked expression on his face gave her a perverse satisfaction. He had no right to ask her such personal questions. After all he was only her hired bodyguard.

"I think it is time to go," he stated. "I have suddenly lost my appetite."

"Well I haven't – no – I want to sample a churro," she insisted obstinately. "I couldn't possibly leave without tasting one."

"I suppose it's in your nature to try anything once," he drawled with a hint of sarcasm.

She ignored his comment, secretly pleased that she had aggravated him. "I'm famished," she enthused.

"Such an appetite for the sensual pleasures," he replied.

"Yes, I'm like the Spaniards in that respect."

"I would say there's a vast difference."

"You mean – no comparison?" she jibed.

"Indeed!"

Starla-sky summoned the waiter for two churros and coffee, before José could protest. She sat back in her chair triumphantly. "So now we have established that I am inferior to you, where do we go from here? I cannot have a bodyguard who thinks he is superior to me."

"What foolish talk," he dismissed airily.

"Why is it so foolish?" she retorted. "Look – how would you like it if I questioned you on how many conquests you've made?"

"That is of no interest. I am a man," he countered haughtily.

"Ah – I get it – double standards."

"No not at all," he answered, still evading the question. "Starla-sky – do you not want to get married?"

"Someday – why – are you proposing?" she quipped.

He pulled a wry face acknowledging her joke. "It is an honourable ambition to become a wife. It should be your main priority."

"Should is not a word in my vocabulary!" she said with contempt.

"It is human nature for a woman to desire to serve her husband and bear his children." He looked at her incredulous, as if she was dim for not knowing.

The waiter arrived with the churros and coffee, stifling Starla-sky's outraged retort. She sank her teeth deeply into the doughnut, with visions of Jose's jugular vein. Not trusting herself to speak she ate ravenously.

"You are hungry. Maybe it's a substitute for love?" he suggested.

Starla-sky almost choked on the doughnut. Taking a sip of coffee, she replied evenly. "I don't need a substitute for love!"

"You have found something to replace it then?" he asked candidly.

"No, I was going to say – if I needed love, I can find it."

"It is not as easy as that querido. Love doesn't happen on a mere whim."

"Oh – and you're an authority on the subject are you?" she replied. "I can take it or leave it."

"Somehow I don't believe you. I think perhaps you have been humouring me. You are a most unusual woman."

And you are an infuriating man, she thought. "I am not unusual. Most women have wizened up these days. Men do not hold all the balls in their court any longer."

"They never have," he smirked. "Women have always been charming but devious. They chase us until we catch them."

She looked indignant. "Then I suppose the woman is so grateful, it is her duty to pander to her man's every whim."

"Si – it is their instinct," he agreed, self-righteously.

"Huh! Your ideals stink – beyond comprehension." She slammed her cup down on the saucer.

"Take care, you'll break that," he said with amusement.

Yes, over your chauvinistic head, she thought furiously. Whether he was attempting to wind her up, it wasn't clear. She was damned if he would succeed in antagonising her further.

"Right – I'm going." She got up, not bothering if he was ready or not.

He gulped down the remainder of his coffee.

Chapter 8

Arriving back at the hotel, they found Aunt Jessie resting, before preparing for the busy evening.

"I'm glad you two are back," she greeted them. "I was getting concerned."

"We've had no problems. It was good to get out" Jose reassured her.

"Yes. We had a lovely swim." Agreed Starla-sky, laying aside her differences with Jose for the time being.

Aunt Jessie sighed wanly and fanned her face with a beautiful, intricately designed lace fan. "Come now, sit down. You haven't yet told me about your visit to the caves."

Starla-sky joined her Aunt on the sofa, leaving the spare chair for José. "Oh Aunt Jessie, it was so exciting. The people, the dancing, the colours – everything," she enthused. "Paco showed me how to dance the flamenco. And he took me to see his grandmother – a most remarkable woman. Anita told me she was the wise woman. Well, she certainly was a character."

"I've heard about the supernatural powers of the gypsies. Has she the gift?"

"It runs in our veins," offered José. "It developed from times past when our ancestors travelled in the wilderness and lived by their wits and intuition."

"If she is a soothsayer perhaps she could heal my aching back." Aunt Jessie winced as she changed position.

"You have a back problem?" asked Starla-sky with concern.

"It's an occupational hazard I suppose. I haven't stopped all day. It flares up sometimes."

"I wish you had told me." Starla-sky admonished, "I would have stayed and helped."

"No love, you're on holiday."

"It will give me experience of hotel work. Besides it doesn't look like I'll be free to do as I please for some time." She shot a derisory glance at José.

"I'm so sorry about all this Starla-sky." She laid a sympathetic hand on her niece's arm. "I hope you won't regret coming here."

"No, it was meant to be," she reassured her Aunt and then shook her head wondering why on earth the realisation had struck her. It was like a sudden flash. She knew beyond doubt, that this whole drama could not be avoided. It was the catalyst to her destiny.

José was looking at her strangely. He then turned to Aunt Jessie. "Rosario – the wise woman, has sacks of herbs and spices – a whole variety of plants to cure disorders. She can provide from her stock anything from a love potion to a remedy for all ills. It is not supernatural, it is natural power," he stressed. "I will seek her advice for your back."

"I certainly will appreciate that," said Aunt Jessie.

"You must rest this evening. José and I will be happy to help downstairs. Won't we José?" Starla-sky said pointedly, daring him to disagree.

"Of course," he replied gallantly.

"Well, if you are both sure? Thank you." Aunt Jessie looked relieved.

Starla-sky nodded. "Okay. I'm going to have a quick shower and change." She hurried out before José remembered his intention of anointing her sunburn.

One hour later, she emerged looking efficient in a sharp black dress, her silken blonde hair secured neatly in a French pleat.

José was standing by the window, waiting. Her heart skipped a beat. He had obviously freshened up also. Gone were the casual jeans and tee-shirt, replaced by smart black trousers and crisp white shirt.

"Are you ready?" She asked breathlessly.

"I'm always ready," he answered, moving over to her by the door. Fresh from his shower he smelt of sandalwood. His shirt sleeve brushed her arm as they went out.

She hurried on down the stairs. He followed, fascinated by her trim form in the fitted dress and the soft skin on the back of her neck, exposed beneath the high piled up hair.

"Damn!" She stopped dead.

José almost fell on top of her. He grabbed her shoulders to stop himself. "What happened?"

"My heel – I've caught it in the carpet," she stressed.

He stepped down around her and bent his head to survey the damage. The stiletto heel was wedged firmly through the carpet into a crevice. "Hold still. I'll see if I can get it out."

Gently, his hands caressed her foot, manoeuvring the shoe. He glanced up at her shapely legs, his breath hot on her flesh. "I suggest you remove your foot," he murmured.

Immediately she slipped out of the shoe and flushed at her foolishness.

José then eased the shoe out easily and placed it back on her foot.

"Thank you," she said flustered.

"My pleasure," he replied, following her down the stairs once more.

She was aware of his penetrating gaze, exploring every inch of her with his dark eyes. So acute were her senses by his touch, her whole being tingled with an odd excitement. Her head was filled with a mass of contradictions.

"Senorita – Thorson!" Luis called out as she reached the bottom of the stairs. "Phone call for Senorita Thorson."

"Oh!" she answered in surprise. Who on earth would be calling her here. She glanced apprehensively at José.

"I will wait for you," he stated.

She hurried to the desk and picked up the phone.

"Hello. This is Senorita Thorson," she said.

"Huh! Senorita is it now?" Came the sarcastic reply.

By his tone she registered immediately it was Matt.

"What do you want Matt?" she asked curtly.

"Don't be like that Starla my love. How could you go off just like that without a word? What have I ever done to you? I miss you."

She had told herself she would not weaken if he should plead with her to come back. Surprisingly, she felt nothing.

"I've been to all this trouble to get your phone number. That friend of yours Laura was no help. However, your Uncle Lawrence gave it to me in the end. He could see sense."

She gritted her teeth. Uncle Lawrence had no idea how Matt had treated her. She never wanted to worry him.

"How's Giselle?" she asked cuttingly.

"Oh c'mon Starla darling. It means nothing to me. We are all free to share our love. Where's the harm?"

Where's the harm?! If he thought that was love, she didn't trust herself to answer. Poor Giselle, she thought. Nothing surprised her about him anymore.

"You know the teachings of my Guru Maharishi-Sapisuitme. We are all one and the same. You really have to find realization Starla," he went on patronizingly.

Oh yes she knew his teachings alright, she thought acidly. The sleaze ball attempted to bed as many women who were naïve enough to follow his every word. The one and only time she had accompanied Matt to one of Sapisuitme's talks, he had made inappropriate suggestions to her. We may all be one in spirit, but we certainly were not all the same while were having our human earthly experience, she construed. No – she would not go down that path with him.

"Actually," she said brightly - something wonderful has happened to me – nothing happens by chance they say…"

"What? What's happened?" he sounded indignant.

"I suppose I should tell you…" she was being deliberately provocative.

There was silence on the other end. He was waiting with growing alarm.

"No – I'm not going to tell you… You know what Matt? You go and share as much as you like!" And with that she hung up.

In the kitchen, an assistant was rapidly chopping salad, sprinkling with sea salt and tossing it in green olive oil.

"Buenos tardes," greeted Starla-sky. "We've come to help. Whatever needs doing – be it preparing food or waiting on tables."

"You are most welcome Senorita. We need all the hands we can get. It's the busy season," smiled the assistant. "My name is Gomez. I know who you are – and of course Senor José."

"Bravo Gomez," José nodded.

"I am honoured Senor." He turned to Starla-sky. "If you are to wait on tables, hanging behind the door is the waitress apron."

"Fine – okay. But first, we would like an omelette please to give us stamina," she chuckled.

"I will make for you my omelette Espanola special – the lightest and best you have ever tasted," he promised.

Starla-sky took down the white frilly apron and fastened it around her tiny waist in an enormous bow at the back.

The aroma of pork fillet, marinating in paprika and garlic, revived José's appetite.

They sat at a large pine table, while Gomez cooked the omelettes and flipped them onto two oval plates.

"That's so clever. I wish I could do that," observed Starla-sky.

"I have been doing this for many years," Gomez informed her.

They finished with a light white wine, whilst Gomez instructed them on how to take the orders.

Starla-sky took the first order. She picked up the tray of food and teetered towards the door on her high heels. Jose watched her go, the bow bouncing jauntily.

Well into the evening they barely had time to think, let alone sit down – back and forth they marched from the kitchen to the dining hall. Federico showed his face from time to time, to see if all was running smoothly. Later, as the pace slackened, Aunt Jessie made an appearance and sat with a glass of wine in the kitchen.

Starla-sky was pleasantly exhausted. The evening had been hectic, but fun. It was time to take a well deserved break. She walked through the bar and ascended the stairs to the living quarters. Taking a cool drink from the fridge, she moved across to the open window for some fresh air. A million stars covered the night sky, positioned directly above, creating a cool tranquillity in the deserted courtyard below.

Music, voices and laughter, drifted across from the town, breaking the silence. Starla-sky leant peacefully against the window frame, breathing in the fragrant air from the jacaranda blossom, mingling with the aromas of spices and herbs wafting up from the kitchen; the sweet smell of lavender, rosemary, cloves and cinnamon.

Suddenly a black Mercedes with tinted windows lit up the road beyond. It cruised silently to a halt in front of the building opposite. A man jumped out. Starla-sky strained her eyes to see. Then she recognised the greased backed hair…. It was Johnny Spears.

As the car sped off, he looked furtively around, and then disappeared inside the unlit building. What was he up to? It crossed her mind she had the opportunity to find out. Impulsively she slipped off her shoes and climbed out of the window onto the flat roof below. Holding onto the drainpipe, she lowered herself carefully onto the patio and took her chance to investigate.

The street directly adjacent to the back of the hotel was empty. Starla-sky unlatched the gate and walked stealthily through the darkness. As she drew closer to the building she stopped and searched for the entrance. The absence of any lighting indicated it was obviously empty. Trying the doorknob she was surprised to find it unlocked. Cautiously she stepped inside, her eyes darting around the room like a fugitive. No one was there. She expelled her breath. Where had he gone?

Adjusting to the darkness, Starla-sky could see she was in a square living room. It must have been unoccupied for some time. There was a musty smell. A door leading to an outer room had been left ajar. She tiptoed across and pushed it very gently. She jumped as it creaked eerily, and then froze at the sound of rustling coming from an adjoining garage. Without warning, a hand grabbed her shoulder.

"Aaah!" A piercing scream of terror left her lips.

A door banged shut and footsteps could be heard running away.

"Are you always so reckless on the spur of the moment – without thought of the consequences?" José glared down at her angrily.

Starla-sky collapsed against him with relief. "José…" she managed weakly.

"Si – you are lucky it's me. What possessed you?"

"I saw Johnny Spears come in here. I don't trust him." She knew she sounded paranoid. "I just had to find out…"

"Find out what? You're being irrational about the man."

"You have to admit it's highly suspicious. He got out of this sinister looking car and slunk in here and…."

"Hear me Starla-sky," he cut in. "Just because you have got it into your head this man is guilty of something, and you have no idea of what – does not give you the right to hound him."

"Well, what was he doing then? Can you tell me that please? You heard him run away, didn't you? And – what on earth are we doing standing here like this arguing about it, when we could have given chase?" She challenged.

His arms were holding her protectively close. She rested like a scared kitten against his chest.

"You are right." He dropped his arms. "It appears whoever was here went in that garage. Let's take a look."

Taking Starla-sky by the hand, he led her outside. They passed a blacked out window at the side of the garage. The door was securely padlocked.

"Well that's that," said José with resignation.

"If you hadn't followed me and made me scream, I could have surprised him and locked him in," replied Starla-sky indignantly.

"And then what? He could be innocent and have a completely rational explanation and you would have found yourself in deep trouble, querido."

"Hmm! We could have at least run after him immediately – I mean, we even gave him enough time to lock up!" She threw her hands up in disbelief.

"Your imagination is running away with you querido. It must be all this drama at the hotel. Anyway I would much rather be holding you close in the dark, than chasing some idiot," he grinned as she looked sharply at him, her face registering surprise. "Come, let us get back before we are caught trespassing."

"Sure," she said reluctantly and vowed to herself that she would get to the bottom of this somehow.

Once inside the hotel, they went straight upstairs to the living room. José did not switch the light on, but lit the ornamental gas lamp. He then took the opportunity to say his piece before the others returned.

"You are not making my job any the easier by your reckless behaviour. Why are you so impulsive? You place yourself in danger."

"I'm quite safe aren't I? And quite cap – "

"Capable of looking after yourself – I know," he finished for her, shaking his head wearily.

"Well it's true," she said petulantly.

"It maybe true in normal circumstances, but things have changed now. You have to accept that. If you don't you are a fool."

She pouted. "How did you know where I was anyway?"

"You didn't think I had deserted my responsibilities, did you? I am aware of your every movement. As soon as you so cleverly disappeared, I came looking for you. I observed the open window and saw you creeping down the road."

"I was not creeping!" she retorted sharply.

He smiled wickedly. "Anyone spotting you would have been mighty intrigued. Waitresses don't usually leave the hotel, under cover of darkness, still wearing their cute little apron. All I could see was that provocative outsized white bow bobbing from side to side."

Shadows danced around the room, distorting his face dangerously. She shivered at the unreal fantasy of the situation.

"I'm going to bed," she said quietly. "Say goodnight to my Aunt and Federico for me will you?"

"Si querido, you've had a hard day," he murmured. "And Starla-sky, whatever else I think about you, I applaud your spontaneity."

Chapter 9

Starla-sky slipped between the sheets and yawned. She was exhausted. The events of the day had drained her and given her much to dwell on. José had proved, throughout their time together, to be changeable as a chameleon. Angry and infuriatingly patronising one minute, the next, gentle, protective and sensitive. It was unsettling to say the least. Best tactic would be indifference, she thought, yes – and anyway Johnny Spears was her main concern right now.

As she drifted off, her mind involuntary somersaulted back to José. She wondered how many points she had scored today and began counting as her thoughts gave way to sleep. Somewhere deep in her subconscious she found herself flying towards him. They came together on the summit of a mountain. It was as if they were on the rim of the world, in a realm of clouds, spiritually united. His strong arms enveloped her. They looked into each others eyes. Gently, he laid her down. The snow was surprisingly soft and warm, cushioning their pulsating bodies.

As time turned night to day, Starla-sky stirred in the half light, lingering between sleeping and waking. The dream had seemed so real it took her awhile to adjust to what was fact and what was fantasy. During sleep, pure peace had permeated her whole being. She was vaguely disappointed. Earth reality was so imperfect and complicated.

The next few days passed slowly. However, no new threats were made to Federico. Nevertheless there was an undercurrent of tension in the air. Starla-sky was becoming increasingly impatient with her enforced confinement. She was like a time bomb ready to explode. Friday could not come quick enough for her. They all agreed it was the best solution for José to take her to the gypsy caves, where she would be safe.

Friday morning Starla-sky said a tearful goodbye to her Aunt and Federico. She was apprehensive of leaving them in this dangerous situation. Although all was quiet at present, she suspected the villains were probably lying low, plotting their next move.

Aunt Jessie hugged her "Federico and I will be okay. We'll feel much happier knowing that you are safe. It's one more worry off our mind."

"Take care Aunt Jessie," sobbed Starla-sky.

"Wipe your eyes dear. Go and enjoy yourself. This is supposed to be your holiday. You didn't ask for any of this."

Starla-sky laughed through her tears. "I suppose one doesn't usually come on holiday to find themselves in the middle of a treacherous plot."

"No dear - José will take good care of you. As long as you do as he says, you will be fine. I think I know you by now Starla-sky – you can be wilful." Aunt Jessie gave her a withering look.

"Alright," smiled Starla-sky. "If you need me let me know. I'll be straight back." With mixed feelings she went down the stairs and into the jeep.

She took one last glance at the hotel, before they sped off along the coastal highway to Malaga. From there, they would take the narrow road turning inland on the way to Granada. José wanted to avoid the normal route.

Eventually, anxiety gave way to excitement and Starla-sky couldn't wait to get back to the hills. Many of the routes were no more than tracks, just passable by car. Sensible people would have kept to the established roads, thought Starla-sky. But no, not José, he had to take the long hazardous way.

He must have read her mind. "Trust me Starla-sky. If by any chance, someone is on the lookout for us, they will never find us on this route."

Starla-sky adjusted her sunglasses. "Is it really necessary?"

"We cannot be too careful," he answered, and then added. "Hold tight."

The jeep started to bump from side to side as the countryside became wild and rocky. Following the outskirts of Granada, the road curved continuously, rising steadily through woods. As the trees diminished in the distance, Starla-sky caught heart stopping glimpses of plunging ravines through the pines. Along the banks grew a bright display of golden gorse blossom. The road widened past orange and lemon groves. In the valleys below a scattering of remote villages could be seen, camouflaged by calm green forests.

Starla-sky heaved a sigh of relief, relaxing at the sight of the smooth sunlit glades. This proved to be premature as the road cut across the Sierras to the caves, winding perilously up through the foothills of the mountains.

José, unexpectedly, veered off in the direction of one of the villages.

"Where are we going?" she asked dubiously.

"I have some business to attend to first," he answered.

They came to an abrupt halt in the middle of the village, outside an Inn.

"We can have lunch here," he suggested. "Come – we will find a table and order before it gets busy. And while we are waiting I must go to the stables."

"Stables?" she inquired.

"Si – I breed horses here."

"Do you? I would love to see them."

"Not today," replied José." You must keep a low profile. Later on, I may take you to see them."

Starla-sky followed him inside the Inn. He greeted the owner and his wife. Then much to Starla-sky's dismay he proceeded to introduce her as a distant cousin from England. He spoke first in Spanish and then in English for her benefit. And, to her alarm, went on to inform them that she was his bride to be. The woman looked unconvinced as she ushered them to an austere oak table by the window.

José ordered for them both.

"What on earth did you say that for?" hissed Starla-sky. "I hardly look as if I'm related to you, now do I?"

"We have to be careful and cover all our tracks. We cannot be too vigilant. I will inform all the gypsies to say, if asked, that you are a relative of mine."

"Won't they question that?" She was beginning to wonder what he would do next.

"They will know it is for a purpose and trust my word."

Starla-sky avoided his eyes. "Why did you say I am your bride to be?"

"An added precaution," he replied off handily. "In Spain it is not uncommon for cousins to marry – especially gypsies,"

How far was he intending to go, she thought wryly. What was it he had said on a previous occasion? Ah, yes – lovers. They may have to pretend to be lovers. Panic surfaced. She had the feeling she was out of her depth.

It was true Aunt Jessie and Federico trusted him beyond doubt. But could she trust herself? He had a dangerous power that could evoke uncontrollable desires within her. It would take all her strength not to dance to his tune.

José stood up. "I won't be long. I will be back before the food arrives. I've told them to bring you coffee."

He left quickly. She watched him through the window as he disappeared up a cobbled alleyway to the stables.

Soon, the woman, smiling broadly, brought her coffee over. "Senorita," she said placing it onto the table. She eyed Starla-sky with interest and pointing to her hair remarked. "Bonito – no Espanol. El pelo inherit de Ingles – si?" she nodded.

"Err – si – that is true. My Madre Ingles," replied Starla-sky attempting to answer in Spanish. She cursed José for getting her into this. At least it was no lie, whatever else he had told the woman.

"Los padres – Espanol y Ingles, hmm!" muttered the woman as she left.

Starla-sky sipped her coffee and turned her head to the window. With discomfort, she was aware of the couple watching her suspiciously.

José arrived back the same time as the woman brought over the meal.

"Ah! Gracias Senora," he said, and then turned to Starla-sky. "Excellent timing. How is your coffee?"

"Its good coffee José," she answered impatiently. "But I feel very conspicuous here."

"Rubbish! You are quite safe. We have covered great distance between here and Marbella."

"That's not what I mean," she whispered. "It's that couple – they keep staring. I feel as if I'm on show."

He gave a condescending smile. "They are just interested, All Spaniards love a romance."

"But there is no romance between us and what's more I am sure they have seen through it." She glared stonily at him. "I wish you hadn't told them that there was. Talk about me doing things on the spur of the moment."

"We had better start to look convincing then." He reached out for her hand across the table. "If you continue to glare at me like that Starla-sky it will not work."

Out of the corner of her eye she could see the starry gaze of the couple. She forced her lips into a smile. José kissed her hand, and then tantalizingly, he turned it over and kissed her palm. On impulse she attempted to snatch it away. He caught it firmly in his.

"Uh! Uh!" He whispered. "Do you want to spoil things?"

She relaxed her tightened fist a little and he squeezed her hand.

"Look into my eyes and show your love, for their benefit."

Starla-sky looked deep into his liquid eyes, a smile curving her lips. "Don't push your luck," she muttered through clenched teeth.

"Ah querido – I love you too," he replied, and then informed her blatantly. "I am going to kiss your luscious red lips now, to prove my feelings to that man and woman over there, beyond any shadow of doubt."

"You dare!" she hissed in alarm.

He dared – and took her breath away. Leaning across the table he gave her a long lingering kiss, full of passion.

Slowly, he withdrew from her and sat back in his chair with a satisfied smile.

She was tempted to wipe her mouth and erase the tingling sensation that he had left. Her lips were full and moist, slightly swollen from the impact. "You're enjoying this aren't you?" she mumbled.

"I can't say it's unpleasant," he stated easily. "It is hardly akin to torture."

Not for him maybe, she thought, and then said. "There are different kinds of torture."

"Si – mental and physical. I hope you will never torture me Starla-sky," he said half seriously, and then added more threateningly. "Don't ever cross me."

She looked uneasy. "I thought I was supposed to be safe in your hands."

"In them yes. But if you choose to go against me –" he shrugged.

The tone of his voice chilled her. "Can we go now?" she asked quickly. "I – I want to see Paco."

"Ah – my amigo Paco – si," he smirked. "Far be it from me to keep you from Paco."

What was he thinking now? She wondered, and chose to ignore his invalid suspicions. However, perhaps it would be safer if he did think her and Paco... Yes, what a good idea. If José was under the illusion that he was going to take complete control of her life, he was mistaken.

José glanced at their empty plates and said brusquely. "We shall make our way to the caves now." He got up and went to pay the woman.

Starla-sky joined him at the door. The woman spoke to José in Spanish, smiling courteously as they left.

"Voya con dios," she called.

"Voya con dios Senora – adios," he answered.

Once outside Starla-sky turned to Jose and asked, "What did she say?"

"Go with God. It's an old countryside saying, when greeting someone or as a farewell."

Jose opened the jeep door for her. "She also said," he informed her with a twinkle in his eye. "She hopes we are blessed with many children."

He started the engine, and then glanced across at her. She blushed with indignation.

"Has your sense of humour left you?" he urged. "Don't take it all so personally querido."

"It is –"she shook her head searching for words. "It's humiliating."

"Where's your spirit of adventure?"

She digested this for a moment. He was right of course. It was an adventure. Perhaps she was taking it too seriously. But that did not alter the fact; she suspected he was taking advantage of the situation.

"You over acted in there," she accused him.

"And you are over reacting," he countered tersely.

"I wouldn't say that."

"Was it so terrible?"

"When you take liberties – yes."

"It was all for a good cause. I have your best interests at heart."

"It was inappropriate. I am selective of who I kiss," she snapped.

"No! I thought you had lost count of your many lovers?"

"Don't twist my words."

"I had no idea I was. But if it upsets you so much I won't do it again – kiss you, that is."

"Fine," she answered. After all, that's what she wanted, wasn't it?

José looked at the road ahead, intent, with some difficulty, keeping a straight face.

After awhile, through a thicket of trees, Starla-sky could see the whitened doors and windows of the gypsy caves. Old men in straw hats, sat in the shade beneath a walnut tree, in idle discussion. Across a spring stood a herd of goats with bells jingling.

As the jeep grew closer to the camp, women and children could be seen gathering fresh fruit, in huge baskets. Ana the cook was cracking olives with a mallet to break the skin. Anita, who had been helping her, looked up as the jeep approached. She dropped what she was doing and jumped up.

"José, José," she called excitedly.

He parked up and got out. Starla-sky stepped down from her side, not waiting for him to open the door.

Anita threw her arms around José. "I have missed you," she said, and then turned her attention to Starla-sky. "I have been worried. Merciful God for bringing you both safely home."

Starla-sky looked surprised that Anita was aware of her predicament.

"It is all right Starla-sky," Cut in Jose. "I told Paco and Anita in confidence, when Federico contacted me. No one else knows."

Anita pressed her finger to her lips. "Not a soul – our lips are sealed. You know you can trust us."

"Of course I do Anita. Where's Paco?" asked Starla-sky.

"He is at the school teaching the children – it is English lesson. He will be back later."

"It will be good to see him," said Starla-sky, suddenly realising she had missed him. He was good company and somehow, his easy going manner managed to lighten the mood of those around him.

"Paco talks about you a lot," replied Anita flatly.

Starla-sky wondered if she detected a slight bitterness in Anita's tone.

Anita watched José lift Starla-sky's case from the jeep. Her face lit up. "Can I help you unpack?" she enthused. "Have you brought all your lovely clothes?

"Yes, I shall be grateful for your help – I hate unpacking," replied Starla-sky.

"You have all the latest styles," sighed Anita enviously.

Starla-sky smiled. "You are welcome to borrow anything you like."

Anita's brown eyes shone with excitement. "I love you Starla-sky – you are like a sister."

"Why thank you Anita. I feel the same."
José had already gone inside the cave. The two girls followed.

He placed the case onto the bed. "Okay – I will leave you girls to unpack," he said and abruptly turned to go.

"Thank you José," replied Starla-sky, looking with amazement around the room. An aroma of herbs filled the air. Pictures above an oil lamp caught her eye. It resembled a sacred shrine.

"Where did these pictures come from?" she asked, her eyes widening.

"They belonged to my parents. They had been packed away for years," explained Anita shyly. "When I was a child, there was always an image like this shining in the night to protect us."

"Who are they?" asked Starla-sky.

"They are the faces of our ancestors. They believed you meet with the saints in a dream and talk with spirits, who cannot communicate with the living during waking hours because there is too much commotion and interference."

Starla-sky looked thoughtful. "I can understand that," she mused.

"We can learn much this way," Anita continued. "The gypsies had their own religion for a thousand and one years. We have always appealed to the divine power."

Starla-sky listened in awe as Anita's face took on a luminous glow. Such faith the girl had, made her envious.

Anita continued in her soft lilting voice. "When I was a child life was one long adventure. I lived in a flourishing magic world of dreams."

"How surreal," Starla-sky tried to picture Anita and José as little children lost in a world of their own.

"At the rising and setting of the sun our elders would enlighten us with the art of translating our dreams. The Romany travellers brought the skill from the mountains of Asia." Anita sat down on the edge of the bed. "Symbols given to us in our dreams were carefully contemplated. Our ancestors understood the eternal laws of the soul."

"Tell me more," said Starla-sky with genuine interest.

Anita looked up at the pictures, and then across to her friend. "There is a hidden knowledge in us that has the power to elucidate our problems, once we are ready to listen to the still voice within."

As the girl shared her poignant secrets, Starla-sky stood in silence, aware of an ever growing closeness to her.

"Why did you hang the pictures?" she asked.

Anita's face clouded over. "I felt in need of guidance. I went to see Rosario because I have been having nightmares. She told me to put seven herbs under my pillow and I should hang the pictures."

"Does it work?" The thought of Anita suffering in silence concerned her.

Anita looked surprised. "Yes, of course. I thought perhaps you too may be having disturbing dreams with these troubles, so I put some herbs under your pillow."

Starla-sky lifted the pillow. "That is thoughtful of you Anita, but my dreams do not bother me." That was untrue, she thought. Her last dream was disturbing. She hoped these herbs would not induce a similar experience.

A shy smile lit Anita's face. "I am glad you are not troubled by nightmares. Can we unpack your clothes now?" Anita was her enthusiastic self again.

Starla-sky observed her with affection. Anita was a mixture of the old values and the modern world. "Go ahead," she replied; marvelling at the fact that anyone could enjoy unpacking a suitcase.

Starla-sky had grown used to the younger girl's endearing personality. Sometimes Anita could be inspiringly spiritual and philosophical, and at other times full of the abundant joys of spring.

Anita sat on the edge of the bed and clicked open the lid. Carefully, one by one, she lifted out the clothes. Dresses, shorts and tops. There was even a bikini which Starla-sky now realised, would be unsuitable to wear. A pair of red calf length trousers caught Anita's eye. She held them up against her.

"Why am I so small," she groaned. "I love these but they are supposed to be short. On me they reach my ankles."

Starla-sky giggled. "Perhaps we can shorten them," she suggested. "I can see they will suit you better than me."

"Oh no, I wouldn't want to spoil them."

Starla-sky smiled at her friend. "I would like you to have them. There's a red top to go with them."

"You are an angel," enthused Anita. "I can see we are going to have fun – but I wish I had your long legs."

"Nonsense - you are perfect as you are – so pretty and delicate. Many girls would love to look like you."

Anita screwed up her nose in disbelief. "Do you think so – really?"

"I don't think so – I know so. Now, try those trousers on."

Anita didn't need any more persuading. Discarding her own clothes, she slipped the trousers on and surveyed herself critically in the free standing mirror.

"Hmm, they are lovely – but on me…?" The trousers hung loosely to her feet.

Although Starla-sky was slim, she was taller and one size larger. "I will alter them for you when we've put my clothes away. No problem."

"I will do the unpacking while you sit down and sew," suggested Anita enthusiastically.

Starla-sky agreed to this. When Anita had packed away the garments in drawers and wardrobe, she sat cross legged on the bed, while Starla-sky finished hemming the trousers.

The two girls were still chatting companionably when Paco arrived.

"Buenos dios Senoritas," he greeted them "Starla-sky, I hear about this problem for Federico - malo! Good you are here now. We take good care of you."

Thoughts of her Aunt came flooding back. "Thank you Paco." His genuine concern caused tears to well up behind her eyes. Her lips trembled.

"Come, come. These do no good," urged Paco.

"I don't believe this is happening," stressed Starla-sky. "It's like something you read about in the newspaper."

"José will not let your Aunt or Federico come to harm," said Anita. "My brother has dealt with far worse than this."

"That is true," agreed Paco. "I can see we shall have to lift your spirits. After I have been to the Taverna in the village with my amigos, we shall dance flamenco."

"I will look forward to that," she replied. "I remember what you taught me."

"Ah! Good. Have you been practising?"

"No, I haven't had the chance."

"Of course you haven't. I guess there's been too much going on."

"Yes that's true. I've not been left alone for a minute," she grimaced.

"So, José has been taking good care of my dance student – guarding her well," said Paco.

Starla-sky pulled a face. "You can say that again!"

Anita looked serious. "It's for your own good," she said firmly. "He doesn't have to do it."

Starla-sky was suitably reprimanded. "I know. Perhaps I should appreciate him more."

"It has been tough for you, I guess," Paco acknowledged.

Outside, the strumming of guitars had already begun. People were beginning to gather around the brazier.

The sewing completed, they went outside to join the others. Starla-sky noticed José sitting alone with his meal. He was watching a group of children singing an infectious ballad. It reminded her of the rhymes she sang as a child at school.

After filling their plates with the delicious food, Paco went over to join José and the girls followed. The children, not being used to strangers, became self-conscious at the sight of Starla-sky and stopped their verse. They were not quite sure of the beautiful fair haired English girl.

Anita started the clapping again. "Don't stop, don't stop!" She encouraged.

Starla-sky smiled and nodded her approval. After much bashful giggling, slowly the children began again. Turning their attention to each other, they gradually became at ease with Starla-sky's attentive presence. As was the habit of children everywhere, once they had a captive audience, their confidence grew. The more daring amongst them showing off and leading the others.

An hour later, when there was no sign of them tiring; Paco announced he was off to the Taverna.

"Are you going to the village de Carlos?" Inquired Starla-sky.

"Si," said Paco. "We go every evening."

"Can I come with you?" She asked on impulse. A drink at the Taverna would relax her and she was curious to visit the village in safety under Paco's protection.

"Why – err – si. If you want to," he answered surprised.

José's disapproving look did not go unnoticed. What objection could he possibly have?

Paco laughed uneasily. "The women do not usually accompany us. But under the circumstances it will cheer you up."

"I think not!" Protested José.

"Why not?" She was defiant.

"It is not the custom in these parts," observed José.

Starla-sky glared at him. He was being ridiculous. She glanced beseechingly at Paco.

He weakened under her stare. "I'll look after her well José. Besides, she is not a Spanish woman and people will understand it is acceptable for tourists. We'll be back in time for the flamenco."

Surely José could not argue with that. To her relief, reluctantly, he relented.

"I will hold you fully responsible Paco," he said formidably.

"Si- you can rely on me," assured Paco as he ushered Starla-sky towards his friends.

She glanced back audaciously at José. She did not like his attitude. Restriction was something she always found hard to bear. It was her nature as a liberated woman to defy anything that was unreasonably forbidden. In her triumph she failed to see Anita's crestfallen face amongst the children.

After their initial astonishment, the young men of the camp were delighted to have Starla-sky's company. On the way to the village de Carlos, there was much teasing and scolding; innocent horseplay. They tried hard to converse with her in a sort of Pidgin English.

Starla-sky had expected at least to see a few women at the Taverna and was a little perturbed to see none at all. At home she had acquired as many boys as girls as friends. She felt at ease in their company and found nothing unusual about it. Soon she was laughing and joking with them all. The young gypsies were captivated. After her confinement with José she felt a sense of freedom. It was flattering. She was not vain, but realised, if she wasn't careful, it could turn a girls head. At least it made her realise there were many men, besides José, to choose from. That is of course if she wanted a man, which she didn't.

They journeyed back to the camp in high spirits, singing at the top of their voices. Starla-sky wished she could join in their Spanish songs and regretted not paying enough attention to her Spanish lessons at school. By the time they reached the camp, she had picked up the catchy verse to sing along.

"I'll teach you our language if you like Starla-sky," offered Paco. "You can come to the school in the afternoons. Soon you'll be serenading with the rest of us."

"Great – it will help me a lot if can converse with the locals," she replied. "Then I'll know if you are talking about me," she teased, and then added. "I must do something in return for all your kindness. I know – perhaps I can help teach the children English, once I have learned enough Spanish to communicate."

"That's a deal," agreed Paco.

Noisily, the young men jumped down from the jeep and went over to dance with the waiting girls. The older women eyed Starla-sky with uncertainty. They did not quite understand her presence amongst the men. Paco had explained to them, she was under José's protection, and they would have to accept without question. Still, they wondered and speculated amongst themselves. Luckily Starla-sky could not understand a word, for she would have been concerned at some of their conclusions.

Happy in her ignorance, she wandered over to the cave, to change into the flamenco dress. Anita, who had already changed, came out, looking a little red eyed. Had the girl been crying? Slipping the dress on, Starla-sky felt slightly uneasy. It was unlike Anita to be so subdued. Perhaps her nightmares were troubling her. She would have to talk to her later and see if she could help. She had great affection for the girl and would be only too pleased to offer advice, and hoped Anita could confide in her.

Chapter 10

The translucent ochre earth glimmered in the firelight, beneath the Anita's whirling feet. She was demonstrating a Paso Doble on her own, beautifully in the centre of the circle. She seemed to be in a world of her own, lost amid the clapping, the strains from guitars and excitable shouts of encouragement. Oblivious to her surroundings, her feet moved gracefully as if taken over and possessed by her ancestors. The centuries slipped back. Her face held an expression of melancholy. It was as if the lunar moon above influenced her.

Starla-sky stopped clapping and watched the girl's trance like state. The beauty of the flamenco never ceased to amaze her. Federico was right, when he said the gypsies were the best dancers. They were indeed the best she could ever have imagined.

José had remained aloof all evening. Not that she was short of attention. The young men of the camp fell over themselves for a chance to dance with her and help her with the more difficult, intricate steps. She was flattered, but at the back of her mind she could not rid the unwanted feeling, that she was admired by every man accept the one who intrigued her.

Unwittingly, she found herself looking in José's direction. It was not as if he was deliberately ignoring her. He had just shown polite indifference. Plenty of dark eyed girls kept him occupied dancing, one after the other.

Much wine had been drunk, well into the night. Stars glinted as diamonds in the midnight sky, silhouetting the dancers gyrating bodies.

It was near dawn when people began to disperse, that Starla-sky found herself by chance, standing opposite José. Without a word and as natural as breathing, they drifted together to dance to the last strains of guitars in the warm fragrant air. The heady atmosphere, brought on by a mixture of potent wine and uplifting music, all contributed to a feeling of being quite unreal and out of control.

José murmured softly in her ear. "You have learnt to dance divinely, in an unbelievably short time." His lips brushed her cheek. Her skin was soft and warm to his touch. "How can a man resist you? It is as if you belong here, mi precioso."

She had tied her hair back tightly like the Spanish women, held in place by an ornamental comb. Her ears were adorned with Anita's dangling antique earrings. She melted into him. He was inducing feelings of bliss in her, a mixture of intense sensations. All the old emotions of falling in love, came flooding back, the agony, ecstasy and entrancement.

Her inner fear and insecurity made her resist with all her might against being this emotional parasite. She was suffering from romantic notions and knew from past experience, it always ended in tragedy. There was nothing more powerful than passion – or debilitating. She thought she was now immune to all this.

José ran his fingers down her spine. "Let us be wild, free and spontaneous," he whispered huskily. "The pine forest awaits the pleasure of lovers."

What was he suggesting? He spoke in riddles. This was dangerous. She pulled away, he was too persuasive. She held his gaze in the moonlight. He appeared like the devil posing as God's gift. It was madness; she must go before she weakened.

"Goodnight Jose," she said firmly.

He let her go. "One day querido…"

She was shaking as she reached the cave and shut the door behind her. Phew! That was close. What on earth came over her out there? And what had come over him?!! All evening he ignores her, and then expects her to fall into his arms and whatever else he was suggesting on a mere whim of the moment!!

Starla-sky glanced over at Anita, who appeared to be asleep. The pictures on the wall illuminated eerily, by the glow of the lamp. Anita must have forgotten to turn it out. Or perhaps she felt safer with the room lit.

She undressed and slipped into bed, beside the sleeping girl. Her eyelids felt heavy. It would not be long before she herself would be asleep. Shadows fell about the room, casting imaginary demons. She was too tired to care. The last thing she saw, before drifting off, was the haunting portraits on the wall. She was unaware that Anita was only pretending to sleep. The girl's pillow was wet from her silent tears.

Activity at the gypsy camp did not come to life until late the following morning. The only early risers were the old women and a few of their men folk. After the previous night of drinking and dancing everyone else had slept late. Friday had now become a special night. Since Starla-sky had her lessons, everyone was keen to demonstrate their expertise.

Despite the lively evening, Starla-sky awakened in good spirits. The herbs Anita had placed under her pillow must have worked, for no dreams had disturbed her. Anita, who was up and dressed before her, brought Starla-sky a cup of coffee.

"Sleepy head," she called playfully.

Starla-sky stretched indolently. "Bless you – you're an angel" She sat up, took the cup and studied Anita carefully for a few seconds before asking. "Are those nightmares troubling you?"

"No. Why?"

"I couldn't help but notice you're eyes looked red last night – and you left the oil lamp burning."

Anita glanced down evasively at her feet. "Oh - I got some dust in my eyes yesterday," she explained. "And I sometimes leave the oil lamp alight now. Rosario said that when the oil lamp is burning by the holy shrine, it dispels negativity. Before I fall asleep I can see the images of my ancestors who protect me till morning light."

This satisfied Starla-sky. She could not challenge the gypsy traditions, or indeed the ancestors. "I hope you've got all the dust out of your eyes," she said with concern.

"I am fine now," Anita assured her. "It's the dancing. It kicks up the dust."

"Ah – I see." She accepted Anita's story having no reason to doubt her.

If Starla-sky's mind had not still been so full of confusion from last night, she might have registered the fact that Anita's eyes were red before the dancing commenced. She was aware however that Anita was not her usual bright self.

"Anita stop me if I'm interfering but I feel something is wrong. What is it?" she asked gently.

Her face held a hurt expression. "It's not fair!" She blurted out impulsively. She bit her bottom lip with uncertainty. "It's just – I'm so envious," she confessed. "I wish I was allowed to go to the Taverna in the village like you."

"Oh Anita I didn't realise…"

"I admire you for having the courage to do as you please. You are so independent. I could never be like that."

"Anyone can be whatever they want to be. Women have come a long way," stated Starla-sky, and then remembered José's accusation. She did not want to be held responsible for leading Anita astray. "Anyway, you are fine as you are. It's foolish to try to change – to be like another. You must be true to yourself. We are all individuals – each one of us important in our own way. Besides, José and Paco know it would do your reputation no good to be seen at the Taverna."

"I guess you're right." Anita began to realise it would be different if she was not a girl from the caves. She shook her head resignedly. "The women talk – they don't understand."

"Don't worry, I won't try and influence them. That would no doubt cause havoc with the men."

Anita giggled. "Can you imagine the men folk having to cook for themselves, while the women congregate at the Taverna?"

"I hadn't thought of it quite like that. I don't want to cause a revolution."

"It will take a lot to change the lives of the gypsy women," conceded Anita. She was aware far more than Starla-sky, what acceptable behaviour was and what was frowned upon in these mountains. "For change to happen too fast – that's if there is to be change – and perhaps there is no need for it anyway – could be dangerous."

Starla-sky gave this much thought. "You're probably right. It's difficult for me to understand. I'm learning though. People are different and your people have a rich culture. There is a lot to be said for their closeness to the natural rhythm of the seasons and the joy in their dance. The rest of us could learn much. Not everyone should be forced to hold the same outlook. Life would become boring."

"I belong with my people. I know they care for me," Anita looked apologetic. "Sorry for my outburst."

Starla-sky swung her legs out of bed and smiled softly. "I'm glad you've seen sense. My Aunt always swore my independent streak would get me into trouble one day."

Anita frowned. "I am sure you have a lot of common sense."

Starla-sky winked. "Even though I feel a little reckless, I'll curb my instincts for today – and right now, what would it please you to do?"

"Right now Starla-sky, I want my breakfast."

"That's the most sensible suggestion I've heard this morning. Come on let's live dangerously," she replied, slipping into her denim shorts and tee-shirt.

Outside, the air was faintly perfumed with pine and myrtle from across the mountains, mingling with the aroma of fresh baked bread, mushrooms and sardines sizzling on the brazier. The earlier cool air that travelled down from the Sierra Nevada's white peaks, had now cleared, heated by the strong sun.

Starla-sky and Anita were amongst the last group to eat. The women and children had departed to the deep pools to wash. The finest spring water welled up from under the crystalline rock, after trickling down from the snow caps, forming clear streams. The gypsies used them for cleansing themselves or washing their clothes.

After they had eaten, Anita took Starla-sky to join the other women to bathe. The area was strictly for women only.

Anita unselfconsciously, stripped off her clothes and immersed herself in the water. "It's lovely and cool," she called to Starla-sky. "Come on in." She began lathering with a bar of crudely made soap.

Some women sat on the rocks naked, young girls with babies and older women, drying themselves in the sun. Others splashed and frolicked in the streams, clearly enjoying themselves. Starla-sky began to feel conspicuous, fully dressed. The pools did look inviting. Urged on by Anita's shrieks of delight, she too took off her clothes, and for the first time in her life, sampled the pleasure of washing in pure spring water.

When they had finished bathing, the two girls sat on the rocks combing out their long clean hair. Once dry, they dressed and made their way back to the camp with the others. Halfway there, the women met up with the men, coming from the other direction, who had been bathing in the large irrigation pond, dug on the mountainside.

José was amongst them, leading a mule with baskets of supplies. Starla-sky's heart began to beat faster. He was laughing, sharing a joke with the men and children, apparently unaffected by his actions of last night. The whole episode had left Starla-sky unsure of herself. Every smile, every gesture he made, she imagined he was mocking her.

The young girls in their party were chattering and shrieking, bursting with their immense energy. Starla-sky stood apart, on the edge of the group, stricken with self doubt. In the stark light of day she realised the intentions José had lavished on her the previous night were no more than a whim, brought on by the heat of the moment. It must have been the wine; the wine and the moonlight gone to his head.

For a fleeting second, she caught his taunting eyes, and in her vulnerable state, saw no love in them. She now interpreted his suggestions as merely following his basic urges. No doubt he deeply regretted it. She was eternally glad she had not succumbed. Afterwards he would have cast her aside disdainfully. With defiance she tossed her head back.

Anita and Paco were discussing the lessons to be taught at the school that afternoon. They drifted on ahead. Starla-sky caught up them in her attempt to avoid José. It was her impression that he had reverted back to his former aloof attitude towards her.

For all José's show of indifference, he missed nothing. "Starla-sky!" he called after her. "I am taking you to see Rosario. Be ready in an hour."

She glanced back over her shoulder. His tone annoyed her. Why couldn't the man be more courteous and ask her if she wanted to go, instead of barking out his order like a dictator?

She tilted her chin. "I'm not sure what I'm doing yet. I may have other plans."

He walked slowly and deliberately towards her, irritation escaping from his mask like expression. "It is more important for us to visit Rosario," he stated flatly. "Have you forgotten your poor Aunt already? We told her, if you remember, we would discuss her ailment with Rosario."

Starla-sky swallowed uncomfortably. She had not forgotten. Indeed Aunt Jessie and Federico were never far from her thoughts. José had no right to suggest otherwise.

"Of course I haven't forgotten," she retorted. "I would appreciate it if you ask me in a polite manner."

"You should know me by now; I always come straight to the point."

"Like a bull in a china shop," she muttered.

"At least you know where you stand with me, querido," he said pointedly.

That's where you're wrong, she thought.

He continued. "I can't waste time. Are you coming?"

She looked him straight in the eye. "Under the circumstances – of course I'm coming." Then as if to win a point, she added. "I'll be ready in half an hour."

"I'll not argue with that. The sooner the better," he said brusquely.

He walked back to lead the mule. Starla-sky turned on her heels and hurried on. Was that what she was to him – a waste of time? Did he find it tedious having to guard her, when he could be occupied with more interesting pursuits? Like indulging his passions with the fiery Marcia. After all, Marcia and José both shared their love of flamenco.

Perhaps, that was probably who he went to see last night, when she was at the Taverna with Paco. How stupid she had been to forget the influence of Marcia. They were a perfect match. Everyone expected a marriage between them. Just because Marcia didn't come to the camp, didn't mean José stayed away from her.

No doubt, he would need a wife soon. Most gypsy men would be married by his age of twenty eight, to produce as many children as possible. Well, that's hardly what I plan for my life, she thought decisively. There is no way I'm going to be weighed down with hoards of screaming kids waiting on him hand and foot. Marcia is welcome to him. And if he has the nerve to think he can sow his wild oats with me, before he settles down…

Chapter 11

Exactly half an hour later, it was a stronger, more determined Starla-sky that met José at the foot of the mountain. He greeted her in a formal detached manner. She decided to steer any conversation well away from too much familiarity. As for last night, she could forgive and forget. He was after all born with the Mediterranean temperament. It was up to her to keep him at arms length.

She followed behind a few paces as he climbed on ahead, up the path. Little was said between them, both lost in their private thoughts, with the soul purpose of reaching the old woman's wagon. Almost to their destination, Starla-sky stopped and looked up at the tangle of coloured mountains stretching beyond Rosario's home.

The old woman herself was sitting where she always sat, under the fig tree, in a meditative state. She was staring straight ahead unfocused on the material realm of being. As José and Starla-sky drew close, quick as a flash, the reality of this world, returned to her eyes. They twinkled as bright as ever. She did not attempt to rise, just nodded a calm welcome.

As they stood looking down at her, eventually she spoke, gazing up at Starla-sky. "You are troubled – danger surrounds you like a black cloak, my Niña."

Starla-sky shook her head. "Yes – there have been problems – at my Aunt's hotel. But – but I should be safe now hidden away in these hills."

Rosario muttered to herself. "La muerte no para."

"What – what did she say?" Starla-sky whispered urgently to José.

His eyes clouded over. "Nothing – nothing of importance," he said hastily, and then explained to Rosario. "We have come to see you on behalf of Starla-sky's Aunt. She suffers pain in her back and we ask if you have a cure?"

Rosario arose from her position. "Come – I give you healing potion for her." She beckoned to them, and walking briskly, led the way to an arched opening in the rock.

Inside, a long wooden trestle table was laden with sacks of mountain herbs. Various plants were hanging in small bunches to dry, or lying loosely on large leaves. Rosario proceeded to wrap some crushed herbs in a piece of cloth.

"This will cure your Aunt. She must heat on stove one day and lay it on her back. Next day dip in ice water, squeeze out then apply."

"Thank you," Starla-sky breathed in the potent aroma.

"It will work," Rosario assured her. "Now sit down both of you, while I invoke protection against evil spirits." She lifted a small cauldron filled with water. "This has been filled at the river, with the current, not against it," she informed them, and then collected together seven pieces of coal, seven ears of wheat and seven cloves of garlic. Placing the ingredients in the pot, she put it on the fire.

Starla-sky and José waited silently, while Rosario hummed to herself.

When it began to boil, she said to Starla-sky. "You my Niña must stir mixture." She handed her a three pronged twig. "Direct these words to your enemies.

Evil eye turn away.
My will excels yours this day.
The power protects me from harm
As I work my magic charm."

Starla-sky took the twig and stood over the cauldron. Halfway through the incantation, her voice faltered as she caught José's eye. He appeared to be suppressing his humour. He probably could not believe she was taking it seriously. Before she had met Rosario and the gypsies, she would never have dreamed in her wildest moments that she would be in this absurd situation.

The thought of what Raymonde and her workmates back home would say if they could see her, almost brought about a fit of the giggles. She composed herself and glanced again at José. No – he was not laughing at her. She chided herself for doubting the power. His eyes held hers with assurance as she finished the rhyme with command.

Rosario seemed satisfied with this and gestured to them to sit down again. "Romany magic never fail, if you are the innocent. Now - restore vigour to your spirits with herbal tea."

She lifted down an earthenware pot, the contents of which had already been boiling with cloves, nutmeg, ginger, lavender and other magical ingredients. After letting it steep, she had added ice to make a delicious cool drink. Handing a cup to José, she then insisted he pass it over to Starla-sky and then repeated the ritual with Starla-sky.

Rosario watched them with affectionate interest. She knew exactly what she was doing. They, on the other hand, had no idea that the drink they were so readily consuming was an ancient love potion.

The week elapsed quickly for Starla-sky. She participated in a haze of activity and commitment. Days at the camp school learning Spanish, were followed occasionally by evenings at the Taverna in camaraderie and dancing the night away. The flamenco soon became second nature. Her greatest wish was to dance at the annual festival in Granada. Each night she practised diligently, praying she would be accomplished enough when the time came.

She knew, the day following their visit to Rosario, José had gone to Marbella to see Federico and deliver her Aunt's herbal cure. On his return, he had laid her mind at rest about their safety. All was well in hand, was all he would disclose. Nevertheless, although he was not forthcoming, she was relieved he was keeping her in touch with the situation.

Even though there was a lot to occupy her, she found it hard to clear her head of José. It unnerved her considerably. However, this evening she was at the Taverna with Paco and something else was troubling her. The bartender, Rodrigo, was talking to Paco in confidence, quietly so as not to be overheard.

Paco had a worried expression on his face when he returned to Starla-sky. "I've just been told that a horseman on a black stallion has been here asking questions – asking if anyone has seen a blonde English girl in the village de Carlos."

Starla-sky caught her breath. "Oh my God – no – how on earth –?"

"I've no idea," cut in Paco. "How a stranger could find this remote place…? We must get back and inform José. Don't worry, no one in village will talk. José has seen to that."

Besides his visits to Marbella, José had been going on solitary walks. On one occasion Starla-sky had seen him in the hills walking in the direction of Rosario's wagon. Another time, on her way to the school, she caught sight of him disappearing into the pine forest. He was acting strangely, keeping an aloof distance.

Shrugging off his indifference, Starla-sky concentrated on her busy schedule at the camp. She remained enchanted by the valley. The spell binding magic of the place enabled her to blank out any unpleasant thoughts. It also had the effect of blinding her to what was happening under her very nose.

Anita, who was usually so full of vitality, had grown quiet and withdrawn. Starla-sky was so involved in her activities that by the end of the day she flopped into bed exhausted. She had not noticed how uncommunicative her friend had become.

The disclosure of the mysterious horseman at the Taverna now jolted Starla-sky out of her apathy. She was forced to acknowledge her predicament. Any moment now she was about to confront José and inform him of the facts. This she was not looking forward to. Paco had driven them back to the camp as speedily as possible.

He was now knocking loudly on José's door. She was wondering how indeed he would react to this new information. He was bound to curtail her activities. She had visions of becoming a virtual prisoner. Perhaps he had gone off on one of his commitments, she thought hopefully.

Focusing her eyes on the whitewashed door, she was relieved when there was no immediate answer. They were about to leave, when the door swung wide. José stood looking at them grimly.

"Buenos tardes," greeted Paco. "Can we talk awhile about a matter of importance?"

Nonchantly, José ushered them inside. Starla-sky had never seen the interior of José's dwelling, which like the others was cut into the red walls of the hillside. The tiled floor was cool beneath her bare feet. He possessed good solid furniture comprising of a sideboard and large table with a couple of chairs in walnut.

Electricity had not yet come to these caves. Starla-sky often wondered if they just hadn't got around to installing it. She suspected it was rejected, for envy of the modern world, did not exist here. Their attitude, she had learned, was one of disdain for the absurd nine to five work that the town folk had to endure in order to achieve their standard of living; lacking any spirituality.

José offered them a seat in the main room, lit by oil lamps. Paco came straight to the point and told him about the horseman.

"So," answered José. "Hmm! This adds a new dimension to the situation."

"Who could this man be?" asked Paco urgently.

"It's highly suspect," stated Starla-sky.

"It is not entirely unexpected," drawled José.

"What do you mean?" Starla-sky showed surprise. "I thought I was supposed to be safe here – well away from the Costa del sol. Out of harms way, you said. No one could possibly find me here," she finished on a sarcastic note. His casual appraisal of their dilemma was beginning to aggravate her.

"No one can get past us Starla-sky," Paco assured her. "You know the men will guard you with their lives."

"But – who knows what this man's game is – what ways and means he has," she said with alarm. "If he has managed to track me this close…."

"Indeed," said Paco. "You have point there. No one more amazed than me that he finds the Taverna. Malo!"

"And how many more of them are there?" said Starla-sky.

José listened to them speculating with patient irritation.

"This ees possible," began Paco. "I – "

"What you are forgetting," cut in José. "Is the fact that if Starla-sky chooses to flaunt herself in the village, she is bound to attract attention – and trouble."

"What!" Starla-sky stiffened in disbelief. Had she heard correctly?

"Did it not occur to you," continued José, "that you would stand out with your foreign appearance?

News travels on the wind from village to village. Your reputation will be embroidered upon and in some cases damaged. I regret agreeing to this. My mistake"

He watched her swallow her obvious fury and resentment.

"That is unfair José amigo," said Paco. "You are being hard on her."

"Not at all," countered José. "If she had not been there no one would have seen her. However, I have faith in you Paco."

"I wasn't seen by the man!" snapped Starla-sky.

"Not yet," replied José with clarity, and then added abruptly. "Tomorrow we go to the Alhambra."

"Who's we?" muttered Starla-sky in surprise.

"You and I querido," he stated.

"And what makes you think I want to accompany you?" she pouted.

"You are still in my charge. If I think it's the best action to take, you must not argue," he said harshly.

"No offence amigo," began Paco, "but I think you are being insensitive."

"Keep out of this Paco." José's jaw was set hard. "You are my amigo, but I must do what is best for her safety. I will not be persuaded to make any more wrong decisions. She needs to open her eyes and see the consequences to her thoughtless actions."

Paco raised an eyebrow. "Are you so sure?"

"Of course," answered José arrogantly. "She lacks the standard of morals of our women."

"Starla-sky is the sweetest and moral person I know," stressed Paco. "She deserves to be treated with respect."

"When she shows some respectful behaviour, then I shall treat her accordingly," José stood up. "It is time for you to go."

Paco arose, roughly pushing his chair back. "You are a fool to yourself José."

"Maybe I have been a fool," José squared up to him. "I am not blind." He looked as if he might strike Paco at any moment.

Starla-sky, who had been listening to their exchange of words with growing alarm, jumped to her feet. "For goodness sake stop this!" she cried. "Whatever it is you are thinking José, you are wrong. And – Paco you are wasting your breath." The last thing she wanted was for Paco and José to fall out over her. "It's alright; I've decided I want to go to the Alhambra with José." She pulled Paco by his arm. "Let's go."

Paco backed away towards the door, controlling his anger. He had consumed a few beers this evening, but not enough to be intoxicated. It was the social side that drew the men to the Taverna, for Spaniards aspire to a dignified disposition and express severe disapproval of drunkenness.

"Buenas noches José," said Starla-sky. "I'll see you tomorrow."

"So be it," he answered.

Starla-sky frowned. He made it sound so dramatic.

Paco stumbled out of the door angrily, without a farewell to José. Starla-sky shut the door behind them.

She clenched her fists at her side and expelled her breath. "That was clever of you Paco," she hissed.

"Is that all the thanks I get?" he retorted. "I'm on your side, believe me. I never realised José was so contemptuous towards you."

"Ha - that's nothing. It was mutual hate at first sight," she spat.

Paco studied her indignant expression. "Is that really true?" His face softened.

She struggled to overrule her latent emotions. "I would have thought it was obvious to everyone. I rue the day Federico made him my bodyguard."

"I'm sure Federico had your best interests at heart," Paco said sympathetically. "Your Aunt and Federico are probably wiser than you realise."

"You think so?"

Paco turned to go. "It is late," he winked at her. "Buenas noches Starla-sky. Sleep well."

"Buenas noches," she answered, absently, a puzzled expression clouding her eyes.

Inside the cave, Starla-sky found Anita kneeling by the shrine in fervent prayer. She almost decided to go out again, before she disturbed the devout scene. Perhaps Anita would feel intruded upon in her intimate moments. Quietly, Starla-sky went through to the other room to boil some water for some herbal tea. Lighting the oil lamp, she settled herself in a chair with the hot drink and mulled over the previous hour or so. Recalling José's infuriating attitude, she silently seethed.

Anita made the sign of the cross and then got into her night clothes.

Taking the last sip of her tea, Starla-sky put the cup on the table, arose from the chair and walked into the bedroom. "I'm so ready for sleep," she stressed.

"I suppose you had a hectic evening." Anita was sitting up in bed solemn eyed.

Starla-sky completely missed the resentment in the younger girl's tone. "Oh – you can say that again," she retorted, her antagonism erupting again at the memory. "Men! I can do without them."

"Is that so?" remarked Anita blandly.

"They make me sick. What's wrong with them?" Starla-sky flopped herself down on the bed and began combing her hair. "First José disapproves of me going to the Taverna – he can be so blunt. Then Paco almost starts a fight with him. I can do without them fighting over me thank you. It's hardly my fault. I didn't ask for any of this."

"No I suppose not," answered Anita flatly.

Starla-sky pressed her lips together. "José is ill mannered and oafish." She swung her hair over her shoulder to one side, and then undressed and got into bed. "I know he's your brother Anita – but sometimes…!"

Anita did not answer. She yawned and lay down wearily onto her side. "Goodnight Starla-sky," she whispered sleepily.

Deep in her own confused thoughts, Starla-sky focused her eyes on the pictures of the ancestors. "Goodnight Anita," she murmured.

Chapter 12

"I feel as though I have been neglecting my duties towards you," confessed José as he and Starla-sky continued along the Plaza Carrera de Darro, in Granada, leaving behind the church of Santa Ana rising from behind dark cypresses. "It appears we can no longer rely on the anonymity of the hills for refuge. And besides, it's unfair to burden Paco with the responsibility of your safety."

Starla-sky took a deep placating breath and clenched her teeth. She had agreed to this outing under duress. It was the only way for her to defuse the atmosphere and keep the peace between Paco and José. If she had refused it may have incited the two men to come to blows. Now, José was implying she had become a burden to Paco. He certainly had a way of twisting words to suit himself. Well, he was not getting away with it.

"Paco does not see my company as a burden I can assure you," she stated

"He is honourable it's true," replied José. "Anyway it's not Paco's business. It's my job to make sure you don't court trouble."

"If I'm such a burden, you can always resign. I'm sure Federico could employ another bodyguard," she returned haughtily, hurrying on ahead up the steep ascent to the Alhambra.

José made no comment, but strolled slowly behind, watching her confident gait; the hem of her long voile skirt, swinging in unison with her sun lightened hair. Wearing comfortable Grecian leather sandals, she was making good progress. However, his strides were longer than hers. He caught up with her as she reached the top of the hundred yard climb, at the horseshoe arch of the Puerto de las Granadas.

"It will do you no harm to visit some of our more cultural places of interest," he informed her patronisingly.

Starla-sky went through the gate beneath deep brick eaves. The indignant retort she was about to make was cancelled by the sight of the Alhambra in sunshine. The red palace – sculptured in sand and water. It was a splendid sight to behold rising from above the woods. Instead, she caught her breath. It looked strangely familiar.

José led her up the Alhambra hill to a stone bridge. She felt the rush of water beneath her feet and stopped to peer over the side.

"The water's so clear," she observed.

"Si – it comes from across the ravine from the Generalife. Its source is the melting snow from the slopes of the Sierra Nevada."

"There seems to be water everywhere. I've never seen so much," she said.

"It was the Moors who brought it here to this parched earth, creating these cool retreats," replied José, standing intimately close to her. "The Moors were obsessed with water – to them it was a glorious delight. And nowhere is its presence so vivid as in the Alhambra and the summer palace, the Generalife above. It is surely the garden of Eden."

Starla-sky watched the narrow stream rippling peacefully below, and then turned to gaze up at the palace. She leaned back on the side of the foot bridge. "It looks magical – like a fairy castle," she said dreamily.

José looked at her with renewed interest. "Why Starla-sky I didn't know you could be so perceptive. I wonder if you really are as tough as you usually appear."

Slowly she dragged her eyes away and faced him. "I'm as tough as I have to be," she remarked.

"And how tough is that querido? What happened to you, to make you so defensive?"

"Just life," she answered whimsically. "Women are tougher nowadays didn't you know? We have attained equality. We can choose to be independent if we wish."

"Ah yes – the modern woman," he said with distaste. He had known women like that in America and found it alien to his traditions.

Starla-sky could sense an argument brewing and had no intention of spoiling the day. She stepped off the bridge and carried on along the central path they had taken through the elm plantation.

"Why, these are English trees," she exclaimed, tactfully steering the conversation to more neutral ground.

"It is rumoured they were brought here from England," replied José. His mood had relaxed.

Eventually they came to another gate at the entrance to the Alhambra. Starla-sky admired the scallop shells above the inner arch.

"An emblem of fertility," murmured José.

"Fascinating," she remarked and walked on quickly.

The courts and halls of the Alhambra echoed with waterfalls, fountains and awe inspired tourists. It struck Starla-sky as an elaborate fantasy. Arches decorated with seashells – patterned stucco windows in each alcove. They walked on white marble floors, between marble columns and paused to admire a centre ornamental mosaic tile.

José raised his eyes upwards. "Look at the ceiling. It recalls the seven heavens of antiquity."

High above, delicate interlaced panels of cypresses and hollows filled with mother of pearl in starry patterns – a work of eastern art. The whole atmosphere had the effect of subduing the usually noisy tourists, to silent interest absorbing the culture.

Starla-sky fell immediately in love with the place. Enchantment and a sense of well being overwhelmed her. The remainder of the afternoon was spent strolling through the complex system of pathways, patios and avenues. Past waterfalls, pergolas, box and myrtle hedges, flower beds and fountains. The scent of jasmine filled the air as José led her to a love-seat in the Pavilion, to rest awhile. She sat and watched the tourists, enclosed in her own private pleasure.

José turned his head to look at her. "You are happy?"

"Yes – I am," she replied. "This place is extraordinary."

He lifted a strand of her silken hair, casually running his fingers along. "You surprise me. I had the feeling you would be bored."

"Far from it. I appreciate beauty," she replied falteringly. The touch of his hand was soothing.

"Andalusians are a people with a natural feeling for art and beauty," he remarked, still stroking her hair softly. "Singing and guitar playing serve two such channels for release." He paused for a second, and then pointed over to the valley. "You see, high on the hill at the last bridge, the path leads to the Generalife in the forest above. It is there that the festival of music and dance is held."

Starla-sky swivelled round. "The Generalife – where have I heard that before?" Somehow it was important for her to remember.

"It is well known," stated Jose.

No – I remember," she enthused. "It was Rosario. Damn! I can't recall what she said."

"She probably told you about the festival," he suggested.

"I don't think so. That reminds me – what was it she said in Spanish on our last visit?"

"Nothing of interest – just an old woman's mutterings," he replied evasively.

"I really would like to know," she insisted.

"You'd rather not," he said mysteriously.

This intrigued her further. There was no way she would drop the subject now. "You must tell me. I don't care how bad it is," she pleaded.

"As you're so persistent," he said in exasperation. "It was Rosario's philosophical ramblings."

"Well – what was it?" she cut in impatiently.

"Rosario said – if you can make sense of it – death stops for no one."

"Oh!"

"There is something else," he began.

"Yes?"

He appeared hesitant. "Forget it," he averted his gaze. "No it doesn't matter."

"What are you trying to say?"

He did not answer her question, and then said abruptly. "Come querido, before dusk we must reach the Albaicin."

His tone was not one to argue with. It would do her no good to question him further. She stood up to accompany him, certain he had been about to ask her something.

Across the Darro valley, opposite the Alhambra, José and Starla-sky sat on the Albaicin hill watching the pink stone of the Generalife turn red-purple, silhouetted against the sunset. Together, in the warm glow, they ended the day quietly listening to the nightingales sing.

In the far distance passed white flat roofed houses and palm trees, Starla-sky could just make out the hill of Sacremente, where the gypsy quarters were carved into the rock, beneath the massive backdrop of the Sierra Nevada. She felt at peace as if she had been touched by a fragment of magic.

José was not unaware of the change in her. He knew the Alhambra had this effect. The building was created for tranquillity. As well as keeping her out of harms way, he had brought her here for the calming influence.

Starla-sky tucked her feet under her billowing skirt and leaned gently onto her elbow. "Romantic Andalusia – the heart of the Moorish kingdom," she stated serenely.

"Si," murmured José. "With one foot in the east."

"When all this is over I shall remember Spain for many things," she mused.

"And what will they be?" he asked.

She smiled softly. "Music - flamenco – singing - sunlight – the rustle of water and the people – bold, witty, with a natural generosity, however poor."

He acknowledged this graciously. "We have our own philosophy in the hills, and reject the materialistic civilisation,"

She was impressed by his idealistic words, but somehow she had her doubts. "That's all very well in an enclosed community like yours. Out there in the material world, one has to strive to survive."

"Ah – because there is a lack of spiritual awareness – corruption is rife," he stated.

She looked at him sharply. "I hope you are not referring to me?"

He leaned back on the hilltop contemplatively. "You are different to Spanish women," he observed.

She shrugged. "Maybe I am. That doesn't make me any less of a person – does it? We are all sisters - the divine feminine."

A few seconds elapsed while she waited for his answer. It was not forthcoming. Instead he said. "I think you are a career woman who has to prove to herself and everyone, that you can achieve – si, an achiever," he concluded.

She had to acknowledge he was half right. It was true she had a career. However, she never thought of herself as a career woman. Even though she had enjoyed working, it was a necessity. "The fact of life is," she began, "one has to work in order to pay the bills."

"Not a woman," he returned sharply. "A woman should stay with her parents until marriage."

She might have known that would be his view. This time she did not react angrily. It was, after all, no more than she expected of him. "A woman should not have to rely on a man to keep her," she argued rationally. "The divorce statistics has taught us we have to be prepared to take care of ourselves."

"We gypsies do not get divorced," he stated proudly.

"In our society we have progressed," she countered. "We can choose marriage or living together. Even living alone and single parentage. It's called freedom of choice."

"How can you endorse such depravity? It demeans the very heart of the family."

"And how indeed do you reach that conclusion?" she wondered.

"If you care to look back over the last decade, you will observe that the downfall of society started when women took jobs outside the home."

"I disagree. There is a balance to be found between a career and motherhood," she replied. "Anyway, what are these women supposed to do until they are married – sit and do needlepoint?"

"It is a career in itself running a home," he answered. "A young girl can learn a great deal from her Mother or any female relative, or extended family in my sister's case. Cooking for instance is an art form. The intricate sewing of dresses is to be admired, and much more."

"Yes – like slaving away over a hot stove, scrubbing clothes outdoors." She lifted an eyebrow with sarcasm. "I suppose you think cleaning and polishing is an art form."

"You have missed the point. Women are created as earth Mothers. A return to valuing them in their rightful place would do much for mankind." He looked at her despairingly. "You have a lot to learn querido."

"I'm learning to take a fresh look at life," she explained. "Women have been suppressed in all cultures for centuries. This is the age of celebrating the rising of the divine feminine. This aspect is in men and women." She didn't expect him to understand.

However, he did. "I am aware querido. This is prophesized in the ancient teachings."

She looked puzzled. "You contradict yourself."

He changed the subject. "Doesn't love and romance change everything?" he asked huskily.

"I'm not looking for that," she replied coolly. "I need to enjoy being on my own before I start a relationship. The only person I have to please is myself and its great."

"But so shallow," he returned.

She inhaled angrily. "To make it in this world, you have to be single minded," she countered. "I make my own decisions and don't have to answer to anyone."

"I suppose having a rich Aunt and Uncle makes life easy for you," he remarked.

"I would hardly say that – I've only just met them, and under the circumstances it's proving to be a distinct drawback, wouldn't you agree?"

"This will pass. What about your parents?"

She was not about to tell him she had no parents and her far from perfect relationship with Aunt Eleanor. "There's no pleasing some people," was all she said.

He detected some family rift and looked at her with curiosity. "Is it perhaps – your parents wish to see you married and settled down," he asked. "My guess is you are a wayward daughter."

"Of course not," she snapped. "My Aunt – my relations, trust me. Anyway, some women think they're only someone if they are attached to a man – and I don't ever want to become like that."

"Strong words," he said seriously. "Do you intend to pursue a career for the rest of your life?"

"If I have to," she answered boldly.

"What about children, don't they figure in your future?"

His casual remark disorientated her. "Well of course I don't want to find myself middle aged and childless. I want children, but I don't necessarily need a man." She was trying to overcompensate for her confusion, by pretending to be something she didn't really feel inside.

Dry amusement showed on his face. "Are you planning on artificial insemination or will it be Immaculate Conception?" he asked.

"What?" she snapped, and then blushed realising her unfortunate phrase of words. "It's far more fun the traditional way," he taunted

"You know what I mean," she answered hastily.

"No do explain – I'm intrigued," he enquired mockingly. He was obviously enjoying her discomfit.

"Well – I may choose, some day in the not too distance future, to have a relationship and if we cannot agree on an equal balance of power – we would be forced to separate."

"And I assume if you should have a child from this – cohabitation – you will not be averse to depriving him or her, of a Father."

"It's not like that these days. It's quite common." She tried to convince him and in so doing, put doubt in her own mind.

Chapter 13

Jose shook his head disparagingly. "Modern intellectual attitudes and the growth of women's lib have broken down the old secure family and religious background." He spoke with fervour. "In so many cases they leave our young people ignorant and defenceless, filled with negative morals. Where does honourable commitment figure in that immature brain of yours?"

She was on her feet abruptly. "Don't talk to me like that!" Resentment creased her brow. "Women's lib was a catalyst – necessary for progress. Women have suffered much through men's physical superiority and domination."

"And they have also caused acute misery to men through their magnetic and emotional powers," he argued.

She was not about to be beaten. "A true balance has to be found, where men and women work in partnership with mutual respect."

The hurt expression on her face made him soften. "Okay, I get your point. I have great respect for women." He attempted to meet her halfway. "Sit down querido – it is good to do some straight talking. I want to know you better."

"You want to indoctrinate me with your views," she replied stubbornly.

"No – I want you to understand," he urged gently. "I want to explain something."

With slight misgivings she returned to her seated position. "You and I could never see eye to eye," she commiserated. "We are light years apart."

He leaned across and much to her alarm took hold of her hand, placing it on his heart. "Does not my heart beat like yours?" he mused. "Do you think I am immune to feelings? I am a man – you are a woman."

"How observant," she said, drawing her hand away quickly, as the first stirrings began to turn her own heart.

"Why so jumpy?" he asked. "A woman with your vast experience of life…"

"Don't make fun of me," she snapped through tremulous lips.

"I wasn't. I find it hard to understand your 'touch me not' attitude, when you have such loose morals."

"Loose morals!" she exploded. "I'll have you know my strict upbringing has given me tremendous self control. Any form of fun was frowned upon."

He looked puzzled. "Is this another of your tales, querido? You forget, you have already informed me of your numerous lovers."

"Oh." She had forgotten how in a moment of anger, her tongue had run away with her that day. "Yes – but I choose who they are. They do not choose me."

"How convenient," he replied sardonically. "No doubt you initiate the intimacy also?"

How on earth had she got herself into this? Her face was flushing rapidly. "I've had quite enough of your insults." She went to rise again.

He reached up and pulled her down towards him. "I apologise. I can see we have our wires crossed somewhere. Perhaps you have not been entirely honest with me. It is foolish to lie. Someday I may get some truthful answers from you – until then you hold me in confusion." He shook his head. "Whoever marries an English woman must live forever in a state of uncertainty."

She watched his eyes darken. He would never marry a foreign girl that was for sure. It would be unethical.

A sudden desire to understand him made her ask. "Tell me – what is it you expect from a wife?"

"No more, no less than she is capable of," he answered flippantly. "Let me explain. You see, the ancient wisdom teaches that a woman's most noble and important function is Mothering, first those in her care, and then in the wider circle. Eventually her love becomes universal."

The jumbled jigsaw of Starla-sky's thoughts began to piece together. It seemed a one sided record had played in her mind for so long, perhaps it was time to turn it over. She found herself identifying with what he was saying. "You put it beautifully," she said. "I guess women have the task of Mothering humanity, giving sympathy and kindness to those in need." Where her words had come from baffled her. All she knew was that the wisdom was essential to her.

His eyes widened. "And from one so young," he mocked. "Ah, but you are right. Are we beginning to understand each other? The Mother aspect nurtures. In today's society this natural instinct is often stifled by intellectual interests."

She fought the battle of conflicting ideas. On the one hand she could relate to what he was saying, but on the other, it contradicted all the modern theories which had shaped her life. "No," she replied. "I don't think we understand each other at all." How could she cancel out all the progress, which had enabled her to experience all the qualities that men took for granted? "There's a whole world of opportunity out there, and I intend to participate."

He was undaunted. "The fact remains that the future of the human race is in the hands of the divine Mother. With her lies the responsibility for the health and well being of the children of the future."

"Such a burden," she remarked.

"With the supportive role of the man, it should not be a burden."

She wanted to ask him if he had ever been in love, but something stopped her. It was best not to become too personal. He had not been forthcoming when she had mentioned Marcia before, and anyway, she really did not want to know.

Much to her initial surprise, she was beginning to see a different side to him. His conduct usually came over as this strong macho male. Today, spending time together in these magical surroundings threw her off balance. Underneath perhaps he was not so chauvinistic after all. He seemed to be articulate and caring. He spoke as one with profound knowledge of the mysteries of life. She searched his eyes for clues to his real personality. He returned her gaze with sincerity.

To him, she was wild – untameable. He saw himself in her. A part of him admired her for breaking down the barriers of convention. This he could not admit, so deep were his beliefs, handed down for generations with the stories of his ancestors.

Mesmerized by his gaze she thought his eyes beautiful, dark liquid – unfathomable and yet she recognised a colourful heritage embedded in his very being. A strength and compassion; an all embracing passionate nature. All these things she discovered and so many questions she would have liked to ask.

He sensed her probing mind and leaned back, resting on his elbows. His long black lashes shadowed his cheeks as he closed his eyes to shut her out.

On impulse she turned onto her stomach, propped her chin in her hands and said. "I would love to know what makes you tick José. For instance – what is your greatest ambition?"

He took a deep breath and sighed, obviously uncomfortable with the question. "Right now it's to sit here and imagine I'm seeing through the eyes of the Moors, when they found Andalusia's golden triangle."

"And what did they see?" she asked.

"They decide it must be heavens floor and paradise is positioned in the sky above."

Her eyes widened with interest. "Do you believe it's true?"

"When I'm sitting here with a beautiful woman – si…"

She lowered her head; her hair fell loosely across her face. "That's a cop out," she replied softly. "I was asking about your ambitions for the future."

"Ah yes – that's a long story and may bore you."

She looked sharply across at him. "Are you implying I wouldn't understand – being a mere woman?"

"The future is our unknowing. The past cannot be changed. I live in the now. Destiny will unfold. What is your ambition?" he asked, turning the tables on her.

"To be good enough to participate in the festival of music and dance," she answered immediately, and then added. "Now it's your turn."

"Okay I'll tell you. But first, if you are so keen to dance, tomorrow we shall pay a visit to Antonio el Garcia Martinez for your audition. The outcome will determine one way or the other. Do you feel you are ready?"

She nodded with enthusiasm. "Oh yes José." The prospect of possibly achieving her ambition, after all her dedication, pleased her.

"Now I shall answer your question. He inclined his head. "I have plans for my people. There is much work to be done. My greatest ambition is to raise them from poverty with education for the children. Then I will be satisfied."

"That's wonderful, but what about your personal ambition?" she asked.

"Querido, I have no need for anything, but to serve my people." With an unshakeable faith he knew in his heart, it was his destiny. "What does a man need besides the mountain air? My needs are simple."

"But surely – " she began. "Does marriage fit into these plans?" It was too late to retract the question. She felt the heat in her face.

He looked at her steadily. "Si – my bride has been chosen."

Of course, thought Starla-sky. He must have made his decision. Marcia must have agreed to set up their life together at the camp. After all, he would not be Starla-sky's bodyguard forever. All this will be a memory and she herself will return to spend time working at the hotel. Later she could continue with her career – perhaps in Marbella. She could perhaps work towards opening her own hair salon. There was nothing to stop her – she was a free agent – no ties. Her thoughts gave way to renewed optimism. She was anxious to know how events were shaping at the hotel.

"How are my Aunt and Federico coping with the situation now, José?" she asked.

Her lack of interest in his former announcement went undetected.

"Don't worry. I have my men scattered unobtrusively wherever your Aunt and Federico go."

"But – have there been any more threats?"

"Not as such. It won't be long before this deception is halted at source."

To question further, she knew, would be like attempting to squeeze water out of a stone. He was obviously not prepared to divulge all the facts. However, she was satisfied that Aunt Jessie and Federico had come to no harm.

"Your Aunt sends love to you, by the way," he added.

Starla-sky smiled. "I shall look forward to seeing her again. Working in the hotel was fun – wasn't it?"

Broodily, José plucked at a blade of grass and considered her question. "Temporarily – si. I wouldn't want to make a career out of it, would you?"

She flicked her hair back behind her ear. "Oh no – I have more ambitious plans," she said in earnest. "I'm toying with the idea of having my own hair salon. I can visualize my name in bold letters above one of those quaint shops in Marbella."

"Hmm!" he grimaced. "A woman boss would not be taken seriously."

She frowned and began picking at the grass in annoyance. "I can see you are having trouble coping with the idea of a woman in the position of authority," she stated clearly. "When will you accept that we want more? It is our right."

"Your expectations are unrealistic," he said doggedly.

"That's totally unfair. No doubt any relationship you have with a woman would have to be on your terms. I suppose it must be very reassuring to be the big man, secure in the knowledge that the woman's main job is looking after you," she replied caustically.

He did not bother to deny this. He found her attitude abhorrent. Also, deep down it bewildered him. "It would be nice to have a woman to come home to," he said condescendingly.

"You men have been pampered for too long," she returned pointedly.

"This is not so," he muttered.

"No? I bet your Mother was subservient," she said with fearless self assurance. "Your future wife has my sympathy." She was becoming dangerously over confident with her words, thoughtlessly disparaging.

He tensed the muscles in his face with displeasure. "You insult me," he hissed, "with your naivety and ignorance. It does not become you querido."

"All I'm saying is that there should be an equal balance."

"And, he will be rich and handsome and you will live in a big house and he will buy you fancy clothes. You only have to click your fingers and he obeys your every whim," he smirked.

"Don't be stupid!" she retorted.

"You must be looking for a fairytale romance querido," he murmured softly. "The man you want is more of an ideal than a reality.

"I told you. I'm not looking for romance," she said tentatively. The way he was looking at her was disturbing. "I'm not a feminist, but that doesn't mean I don't want to be treated as an equal with men." She sounded breathless. He had obviously upset her.

Unconsciously she longed for a soul mate to complete her. Take away her loneliness and insecurity – give her peace and the love she lacked. But in reality relationships are challenging. They give the greatest lessons in life and also have the potential to enhance happiness. Besides sharing adventures together, it was the simple pleasures she craved. She wanted romance, walking hand and hand by the sea, visiting art galleries, conversation over lunch, laughing, singing, and hugging. Someone to hold her when she was sad and tell her everything was going to be alright.

Darkness was beginning to close in. Lamps came on amongst the greenery, creating a landscape of haunting beauty. Starla-sky sat subdued under the stars and watched the clouds dance in the wind around the crescent moon. The night air carried scents of flowers from market gardens across the ravine of the Darro River.

José could smell the perfume on her skin. To him she looked wide eyed and vulnerable, her full lips pouting provocatively in deep thought. On impulse he kissed her lightly on the cheek. "I'm sure the man who wins you will spoil you and love you and be prepared to give his life for you," he said softly. The touch of her skin aroused deep feelings in him.

The temptation was too great for his passionate nature. He leant across and progressed hungrily to her lips. Her breath was coming in short gasps. She felt weak. It was not like her at all.

He pulled away slowly. "Don't be afraid," he soothed, stroking her arm consolingly. "My guess is, for all your bravado, dealing with your emotions is difficult for you."

The delicious heat of his kiss left her stunned. She could barely speak. Her mind was in turmoil.

"We had better go before we do something we may both live to regret," he said gently, taking her arm to escort her back down the hill.

He would find it hard to adjust to this new kind of woman. Somehow she posed a threat to his manhood. The world was changing too fast for him. He clung to the old beliefs and customs with a vengeance as if his very life depended on it. Who was this new breed she represented? It was alien to the very chore of his gypsy soul.

Chapter 14

Antonio el Garcia Martinez was a man with an incurable addiction – women. And the more unobtainable they were the more he took delight. A wealthy self made man of some standing in the world of music and dance at Granada; he indulged in the pleasures of life to an incredible excess. Although overweight, he still possessed a full head of coarse black hair and moustache to match. Like José, he was unusually tall for a Spaniard, and one could tell he had once been quite good looking.

His wife, a rotund bustling woman, turned a blind eye to his infidelities and compensated by being kept in a life style of luxury.

Marcia was the apple of her father's eye and since the day she was born nothing had been too good for her. She had come to expect to be granted whatever she desired. Second best just would not do in her eyes and the biggest catch of the moment was José Velázquez.

Starla-sky sat beside José in the high ceiling room, her heart palpitating with anticipation as she waited to be auditioned for the festival of music and dance. At the sound of approaching voices, she stood up confidently, assuming a brave face. Inside she was quaking with nerves and excitement. A sense of inadequacy brought butterflies to her stomach.

Outside, the conversations grew nearer and louder, until the door swung wide and with a theatrical flourish a flamboyant Antonio entered the room. He greeted José with affection, and then turned his concentrated attention towards Starla-sky,

"Ah – perfecto," he gasped, appraising her from head to foot. He turned to José and winked. "How you say – a decorative piece."

José gave his friend a good humoured, reproachful stare. "This is Starla-sky," he informed him, and then added. "You are still an audacious rogue Antonio."

"Si! There is no reason to be bashful in coming forward in order to appreciate one of mans most basic pleasures. The opposite sex, when put together like this pretty creature…"

Starla-sky squirmed as he introduced himself by embracing her bodily. He held her a little longer than was necessary. His manner she disliked intensely. She did not appreciate his sexist humour, especially when it was targeted at her.

To José, he was a trusted mentor and although Antonio was apt to make lewd comments, it was just his bawdy way. The plus side of his character was his loyalty to his friends, if not his wife.

Starla-sky was aghast as to what she had let herself in for. Before she could change her mind, Antonio took hold of her by the arm and whisked her into a large studio.

"I am impatient," he announced loudly, "to see this beauty in action."

The studio was empty, except for a long cushioned bench and music equipment. José sat down while Antonio summoned his guitarist. Starla-sky stood proudly in the middle of the polished wooden floor, attempting to bite back her antagonism.

Without warning the music started and Antonio indicated for her to begin. With determination she went through the steps, remembering all Paco had taught her.

"Charming," commented Antonio. "Is it not desirable José that women want to please us – perform for us? I like the way her hair is arranged coquettishly, plaited and adorned flirtatiously with the pink orchid. I look for all these touches when grooming my dancers"

Starla-sky gritted her teeth and launched herself into a state of wild stamping frenzy. If she had not been so intent on acquiring her dance ambition, she would have taken great pleasure in slapping Antonio's face and storming out. Instead, the dance gave her the opportunity to release her anger, into a climax of abandon. Her explosion of feelings only caused Antonio to applaud her furious passionate performance.

José was silently watching every movement of her body in the fitted flamenco dress, an extravaganza of black magic and palest pink taffeta. The seductive bodice had looked perfect when she had tried it on this morning, but as she danced it became apparent she was in danger of revealing too much.

Ignoring Antonio's x-ray eyes, she was well aware of the effect she was having on José. Against all her principals she had to admit she was enjoying dancing every movement for his admiration.

"It is one of my fantasies to see a woman perform the flamenco naked," drawled Antonio. "I can imagine it would be the most exciting performance of my life. Especially if it was one as voluptuous as her. Don't you agree amigo?"

José loosened the neck of his bandana. "That – I doubt amigo; you will ever have the pleasure." He spoke lightly, and then added with slight irritation in his voice. "Her name is Starla-sky. Please refer to her as such."

Antonio bellowed with laughter and slapped José on the knee. "Do I detect more than a passing fancy for the girl?"

"She is good dancer, I think – and deserves respect," answered Jose, evasively.

Antonio assessed him shrewdly. "Then, I offer my apologies. But don't let Marcia hear of this."

José shrugged.

"Hmm! I can see Starla-sky," continued Antonio, emphasizing her name, "has a certain allure. It is obvious she is not one of your little gypsy girls you bring to me for dance approval."

"No she is not," replied José curtly. "Of course I have always appreciated your vast experience of the flamenco. I would not dream of allowing any dancer to join my troupe for the festival without your approval."

"You flatter me amigo," remarked Antonio, and then clapped his hands for the music to cease.

Starla-sky stopped abruptly in the middle of a Paso doble.

"I am impressed," appraised Antonio. "Starla-sky will be a valuable addition to your dancers José." He arose, walked over to her and lifted her chin. "Such unique beauty." He traced a finger down her bare shoulder. It did not occur to him to conceal his lecherous pleasure. "The softest skin…" he said.

Starla-sky flinched and turned her cheek away from him.

"A frosty exterior I always find hides a frisky nature," he proclaimed. "It would excite me to tame you wild one."

"It would take more than a snake like you," she spat vehemently, no longer able to contain her anger.

He threw his head back and roared with laughter. "Ah! You are one lucky man Jose."

Starla-sky waited with interest for José's response. Before he could answer, the door flew open and Marcia made an elaborate entrance. The merest glance was afforded towards Starla-sky. She advanced purposefully across the room to José and flung herself into his arms with a barrage of excitable Spanish.

Antonio watched Starla-sky with a wry smile, waiting for her reaction. She maintained her dignity. After all, she was fully aware of José and Marcia's intimate relationship.

Marcia released José and smiled as she did a twirl for his benefit. From the limited Spanish Starla-sky had so far acquainted herself with, she gathered Marcia had been clothes shopping and was seeking José's approval. He nodded admiringly as she pirouetted before him.

Starla-sky tightened her jaw. There was no denying Marcia looked stunningly elegant. The black silk frilled blouse co-ordinated stylishly with her wide black palazzo pants. The cut of the material was obviously haute couture. Her raven curls were arranged on the crown of her head in contrived sophistication. The beautiful dark eyed girl draped her arms possessively over José's shoulder. She did not once acknowledge Starla-sky's presence, but spoke with humourless tone to her Father. It was apparent she was displeased.

Antonio answered angrily with a severity that astonished her. Marcia's lips quivered, more with fury than fright. Then her eyes narrowed, focusing on Starla-sky; her face fixed in an angry glare.

José gently unwound Marcia's hands from his shoulders and said to Antonio. "We shall not take up any more of your day. I'm sure you have things to attend to." He glanced at Starla-sky, and then added. "We both agree that Starla-sky is expert enough to perform. Thank you for your time amigo."

"It was my pleasure. I am only too pleased to be of service," replied Antonio. "I leave the final decision, as always, to you."

José guided Starla-sky by the arm towards the door. "She is ready – Starla-sky has passed the audition with a credit," he smiled.

Once outside, Starla-sky heaved a sigh of relief. The whole episode with the nauseating Antonio el Garcia Martinez and his equally unpleasant daughter Marcia had been a tremendous ordeal.

José had driven them nearly halfway back, before Starla-sky's rage erupted. He knew she was angry by her stony silence. Eventually he remarked. "That wasn't too bad, was it? You passed with flying colours."

Starla-sky stared at him in disbelief. "Not too bad!" she shrieked. "Not too bad! Do you realise I've just been the victim of sexual harassment. That – that obnoxious man!"

"Come now, don't be so sensitive. Antonio finds you attractive. He likes to show his feelings. Certain men of Spain are not predisposed to restraint."

"Insufferable!" she exclaimed. "How could you expose me to such a rude and vulgar man?"

José studied her indignant face. "You handled yourself very well, I thought."

"Hmm!" she pouted.

"Look – I know Antonio. He means no harm – he's a good man. A bit exuberant maybe – si," he shrugged.

"I pity his wife," she retorted.

"There's no need – his wife is very well looked after."

"Oh yes – turning the proverbial blind eye," she conceded dryly.

"I do not condone his behaviour." José raised his hands from the steering wheel. "Starla-sky querido – will you never understand?"

"No – no I don't think so," she answered soberly, her lips beginning to tremble with bruised pride. Of course José would stick up for Antonio, wouldn't he? After all they were soon to be related.

Early evening, Paco joined Starla-sky around the brazier. By now, she felt a growing satisfaction about her achievement and a sense of belonging among the dancers.

Paco was eager to know how she had got on. His excitement matched hers.

"Tonight we celebrate at the Taverna," he declared.

"Yes," answered Starla-sky enthusiastically. She then glanced around warily for José. It crossed her mind that Paco was being deliberately defiant after his disagreement with José the other night.

José had disappeared already. He had told her he was going away on business for awhile and urged her to spend her time practising her dance routine for the coming festival. He had this infuriating habit of leaving without telling anyone. She shrugged. Well – he could not stop her doing what she wanted. No possible harm could come to her with Paco and the boys.

Piling into the back of the jeep in high spirits, Starla-sky caught sight of Anita standing forlornly in her doorway. As they left, she watched Anita's figure diminish smaller and smaller. The girl then turned and went inside.

A pang of guilt dampened Starla-sky's jubilation. It was one thing to thwart José's repression, but she had no wish to antagonise Anita. Still, sometimes one has to make a stand for what one believes in, she thought.

In this frame of mind she entered the Taverna. Paco ordered champagne and Rodrigo placed a small saucer of basic tapas with olives on their table, as accompaniment. When told that Starla-sky was now an accomplished flamenco dancer and would be performing at the festival, Rodrigo vanished out the back and hastily returned with a platter of hot prawns in garlic. He spoke a few words in Spanish to Paco, which Paco duly translated.

"He says – in honour of our English friend. We appreciate that you put yourself out to learn the dance that is nearest to our hearts."

Starla-sky smiled at Rodrigo graciously. "Mucho Gracias," she said, and then turned to Paco. "Tell him I am the one who is honoured to be accepted."

"Tell him yourself. Now's your chance to practise your Spanish and see how you are progressing with the lessons," suggested Paco flippantly. With his head on one side he grinned mischievously.

Not one to be out smartened she attempted to answer Rodrigo in her faltering Spanish. The men applauded loudly her endeavour. If her unpolished accent assaulted their ears, they did not show it.

Paco poured another glass of champagne. "Did Antonio give you a hard time?" he asked inquisitively.

She narrowed her eyes at the memory. "Words fail me Paco."

"That bad eh?"

"I can't tell you..." she shook her head, "his boorish innuendoes…"

"I know he has a reputation with the ladees."

"Thank God I won't have to audition for him again."

Paco's face darkened in anger. "I suppose José did not defend you. He is challenging my friendship to the limits."

"Well – José did stand up for me." She acknowledged José had put Antonio tactfully in his place.

"Anyhow!" exclaimed Paco. "You shall partner me for the festival."

"What about Anita?" she asked. "Don't you usually partner her?"

"We've discussed it and as it's your first performance you will dance with me – your teacher. José of course partners Marcia. Anita will dance solo this year."

"In that case I shall be happy to accept."

Time passed quickly in a flurry of activity. Starla-sky was never far from Paco's side. The routine they were perfecting for the festival and her Spanish lessons took care of that. She was so determined not to let the others down; she was oblivious to all but the dance. Paco grew to be a close and trusted ally.

José had not returned and she saw no reason to stay away from the Taverna. To the extent of her knowledge, no more sightings of a suspicious nature had been reported. Whoever had been looking for her had clearly made a fruitless search and gone elsewhere.

The day before the festival, Starla-sky was choosing which dress to wear. Paco had been so generous, allowing her complete access to his Mother's flamenco wardrobe. She smiled recalling his words. "My Madre would not want these works of art to go to waste and lay idle," he had said. "I somehow feel she would approve of their wearer."

"It's lucky they're my size," she had enthused.

Appraising each dress individually, she came across a glittering electric blue and silver number of unique appearance. Immediately, she knew this was her choice. Carefully slipping it on, she was pleasantly surprised. It fitted like a glove. Scrutinising herself in the mirror, she observed the bodice encased her securely. In her excitement she rushed out of Paco's dwelling, to find Anita and ask her opinion.

"Anita," she called. "Look - what do you think?"

Anita was standing outside watching the children play. She glanced in Starla-sky's direction and said in a toneless voice. "You look beautiful."

Starla-sky was aware that something about Anita was not as she had expected. The usual smile that greeted her was absent. The last time Starla-sky had seen Anita, she had not been like this. Or had she? Starla-sky had been so busy she could not remember.

"Oh – Anita – you think I should wear this one tomorrow?" she asked hesitantly.

Anita leant back against the wall and stared into space. "Why not? You always outshine every else anyway," she replied with an edge of bitterness. "Why bother to ask me?"

Her elation suitably squashed, Starla-sky eyed her friend with compassion. "I – I just thought you might be happy for me. What's wrong?"

Anita shrugged. "Nothing," she replied and continued staring into the distance.

Something was obviously very wrong. It was as if her spirit had finally broken and left an empty shell.

Starla-sky had never seen her like this before. In desperation she tried to cheer her up.

"Just think Anita. Tomorrow we shall be dancing at the festival. Aren't you looking forward to it? Paco has been wonderful – he gives me so much confidence. Thank you for agreeing to let me partner him…" she trailed off.

By the angry look on Anita's face as she turned to face her, it was plain Starla-sky had said the wrong thing. Anita looked just like José when he was about to explode.

"I agreed to nothing. As usual I was told. It was assumed good little Anita will do as she's told." She blurted it out, her voice shaking. Tears began to roll helplessly down her cheeks.

"Oh Anita please don't cry. It's not like that I'm sure." Starla-sky stepped forward to console her.

"I don't want your pity," Anita choked with fury. "Leave me alone – go – just go." She stumbled through the door and slammed it loudly.

Starla-sky stood in stunned silence. She contemplated following her friend inside, but reason told her this was the last thing Anita wanted. In her present mood there was nothing she could say. She wondered if it had been her own influence on Anita that had caused the outburst.

Slowly she walked back to Paco's cave and removed the dress. She hung it carefully on the rail and put her own clothes on. Somehow it did not seem important anymore. Paco would not be back till much later. This gave her breathing space to think clearly. Her spirits had plummeted, bringing her down to earth with a bang. Anita's increasing unhappiness had been happening right under her nose and she had been too self absorbed to notice. How could she have been so stupid? She would leave Anita to cool down and then go and see if she could sort things out.

A few hours later, a subdued Starla-sky cautiously opened Anita's door. There was no sign of the younger girl.

"Anita," she called gently. There was no response. Starla-sky assumed she had gone for a walk.

Stepping outside again, she glanced around the camp. Suddenly, far in the distance, she glimpsed Anita on the path up the mountainside, heading towards Rosario's.

Chapter 15

Starla-sky tried to pinpoint the exact moment her life changed. That evening she had visited the Taverna as usual and later when she eventually retired to bed, Anita was fast asleep. Realising her friend had deliberately avoided her all day, she sighed with regret as she settled down between the sheets.

It was not long after Starla-sky drifted off into a troubled sleep, when she was awakened by the sound of a distant shotgun. With a jolt, she sat upright. On impulse, she quietly crept out of bed and observing Anita was still sleeping, draped a black shawl over her head and stole out to investigate. No one else in the camp stirred.

Becoming accustomed to the moonless night, she made for the mountains in the direction of the shotgun sound. Under cover of darkness, she thought herself safe. The road curved upwards, around a steep slope. Beneath her it descended lower towards the valley floor. High on the mountainside surrounded by meadows and trees, she stopped and caught her breath, rigid with fear.

A great shining horse – a Spanish pure blood, stood before her. The magnificent beast whinnied and swished his tail as its rider urged it to cantor onwards. Was this the man who had been tracking her? The man who had been involved with threatening Federico and her Aunt? She had to find out. Anger replaced her fear as she vowed to expose him. Following in his direction up the mountain pass, listening for the click of hooves as she went;

all the frustration of her eventful day and thoughts of Aunt Jessie's anguish urged her on.

After a while she became aware that the clicking of hooves had stopped. As she looked up, a clearing came into view. She straightened – it was now or never. Later she wondered if it was stupidity or a super human courage that stilled her fear and made her ready to challenge the rider.

Sensing the intrusion he spun round. Dressed in black, mounted high above her on the stallion, proud and arrogant like a nobleman from some Gothic novel.

"Parar!" he bellowed into the blackness of the night.

Starla-sky knew the sound of that voice only too well. "José!" she gasped in astonishment.

"What in God's name are you doing here Starla-sky?" he demanded huskily. She had never seen him so angry.

"I – I heard a shot and thought –"

"How could you be so foolish," he cut in. "You place yourself in grave danger. All the trouble I have been to, to keep you safe and you repay me like this. You make a mockery of my protection." He noticed her glance quickly at the shotgun glinting on his saddlebag. "No – it wasn't me that shot the gun," he answered her inquiring gaze. "I had the culprit in my sight – when you appeared. Madre de Dios, I could cheerfully shoot you instead."

With ease he dismounted and strode towards her.

"What - are you going to do?" she whispered with growing alarm.

"What I should have done a long time ago." He took hold of her by the shoulders and shook her violently. "It's time someone made you realise the danger you are in."

As she struggled, he loosened his grip. "It won't be you – I can assure you," she retorted defiantly.

"Well if it's not me, perhaps your conscience will make you see sense," he barked.

"What do you mean?"

"Are you blind? Can't you see what you are doing to Anita? I came home this evening and find her in tears. I have been told you have frequented the Taverna. I advised you not to go there again, remember?"

"Is that your final word?" she returned haughtily.

"No it is not," he answered. "It seems – you are so intent on enjoying yourself, you trample on the feelings of others. Don't you know Anita is in love with Paco, her heart is broken? You show blatant disregard for her feelings. Have you no shame?" Eyes blazing he grabbed hold of her again, digging his fingers into the flesh of her shoulders.

"Stop – you're hurting me," she cried.

To add insult to her injured feelings he pushed her away disdainfully. Through her hurt and distress, she was aware of her own guilt. Anita in love with Paco? Of course, she should have known. How could she have been so unaware? In her bid to prove her independence to José and perhaps make him jealous, she had completely overlooked Anita. It was time to call a halt to this charade.

"There is nothing but friendship between Paco and I," she stressed. "It is possible for a man and a woman to have a platonic relationship you know."

"Don't play games with peoples emotions Starla-sky," he warned.

What did he mean? It was him playing with her emotions. In his present state explanations were impossible. She turned and attempted to leave. Quickening her pace, she tried to put as much distance between them as possible.

He had other ideas. With one fell swoop he swept her up into his arms and expertly threw her bodily onto the horse. She struggled into a seated position and glared at him.

"How dare you!" she spluttered.

Mounting behind her, he crushed her forcibly against his chest and took hold of the reigns. "I'm taking you back before you cause any more havoc."

"You can't do this to me. I'm a free agent," she shrieked. "God, I wish I was a man."

He gave a short laugh. "Freedom is a two edged sword," he replied with some irony, and then added. "Perhaps you should have been born a man querido. Then at least I could challenge you to decent fist fight. But, as it is, if you continue to flout my judgement, you leave me with no choice…"

What he meant by that, she dreaded to think.

Life was never quite the same for Starla-sky after that night. She was forced to admit, if it had not been for José's accusations, she might have continued to go on in her carefree way, oblivious to the implications. Her eyes had been opened; a change of outlook was called for. Not towards José, she hastily construed, but for the sake of Anita.

When she awoke next morning, Anita was already up and gone. Before the onslaught of preparations for the much celebrated festival, which was due this afternoon, Starla-sky was determined to see Paco and broach the subject of Anita. It was time to put things right. She threw on a floaty purple Indian cotton sundress, drank a quick cup of coffee and then went in search of Paco.

The early morning mist rose over the hills, obscuring the view she had taken last night. Straining her eyes, she sought his familiar face. At first she couldn't see him. In the opposite direction, voices came from beside the brazier. To her relief, amongst the chatter, she heard Paco's unmistakeable laugh. The group were having an excitable discussion about their dance routines. She waited until most of the gypsies had drifted off, before she tapped Paco lightly on the shoulder.

"Hi Paco," she greeted him, and then said more seriously. "Can I speak to you alone for a minute?"

He turned to face her. "Sure Starla-sky," he grinned and put his hand on his heart in mock dismay. He lowered his voice. "Am I guilty of some dark and terrible deed?"

"No," she replied. "I want to talk to you about Anita. Have you noticed how unhappy she's been lately?"

His jovial expression changed. He shook his head with a mixture of disappointment and acceptance. "I told you it was inevitable – she would soon get bored with the restrictive way of life here for gypsy women. I guess she's yearning to return to the excitement of America."

"You've got it wrong –" Starla-sky tried to tell him.

"Let me finish. I will tell you something," he confided. "She belongs to my heart and always will. I love her – there – I've confessed. But it's no use, I can't hold her back. I had plans – I was waiting until she was a woman – mature enough to marry." He stared at the ground sadly. "Remember that time I took you to Rosario? – well – she told me to curb my tongue and watch my actions as unintentionally I would end up hurting the woman I love. I knew then that if I told Anita I loved her, she would be torn between staying with me out of pity and returning to America."

"No Paco, listen to me. Anita – "

At that moment the guitarists chose to interrupt with the tuning of their guitars, in readiness for later. They began singing loudly. Dancers appeared from out of nowhere eager to practise their routines, inviting Paco's approval. Further conversation was impossible. It would have to wait, she decided. The men were surrounding her urging her to dance, when a hand grabbed her by the arm and pulled her away.

"Is no man safe when you're around?" snapped José.

"What!" she exclaimed. His ludicrous assumption was laughable. Was this his dry sense of humour? "You're insane,"

"I can't leave you for a moment. You're beauty incites them to make fools of themselves."

She gave a short laugh. He could not be serious. It amazed her that he saw her as some femme fatale. "The only fool around here is you," she replied bluntly.

"That remains to be seen," he returned, and then continued. "I came to find you, to show you what I found this morning – come!"

Out of curiosity, she followed him to the door of his cave. There, sprawled on the dusty ground, lay, what was once a beautiful eagle owl.

"Oh! The poor creature," she gasped.

"This – was the shot you heard last night," he informed her. "I found it in the hills."

"Who would do such a thing?"

"Probably some idiot – for the sheer hell of it."

She looked aghast. "But, you must have some idea? You said you were following a man on a horse last night."

"I was – but thanks to your interference he escaped."

She knelt to stroke the feathers of the bird, hiding her remorse. It was her fault that the man got away. It was her fault Anita was broken hearted. If she had not been so wilfully intent on doing her own thing, to prove a point, and perhaps respect their customs a little more – José probably would have caught the villain by now. No man could hope to outwit him. She felt fully responsible.

"Where's your horse?" she looked up at him, the sun making her squint.

"He's tethered in the pine forest. I intend taking him back to the stables this morning. I suggest you stick close to the camp until you all leave for

Granada. Stay with the women – they can help you to get ready – familiarize you with the procedure."

"Yes – that's what I planned to do," she endeavoured to sound reasonable.

"Make sure you do," he replied firmly. He bent to retrieve the bird. "First, I will dispose of this. I'll see you at Granada." And with that he turned swiftly on his heels, before she had time to reply.

She wanted to ask him what he was going to do with the carcass of the bird. At least she hoped he would give it a proper burial. Would he have ridiculed her wish as foolish sentimentality, she wondered?

The morning proved pandemonium. There was great excitement among the gypsies. An early lunch was followed by a bathe in the stream. Starla-sky accompanied the women and Paco joined the men. An opportunity to converse with him, did not crop up. Anita made a brief appearance to wash – sought Starla-sky out and whispered an apology for her previous outburst.

"Please forgive me – I had no right," she confessed.

"There is nothing to forgive," answered Starla-sky. "It's me who should apologise."

Anita kissed her quickly on the cheek, then turned and ran back to the camp. It was so true of Anita's character to forgive so readily, thought Starla-sky.

In volatile spirits the gypsies returned to their caves to make ready for the festival. Inspired by what was to come, one by one, they spilled out into the afternoon sunshine, adorned in their spectacular finery. All this was conducted with a great deal of noise; reacting with good humoured shouts and shrieks, quick to catch each others compliments.

Starla-sky had delayed putting on her dress and was busy making herself useful. She was fixing the women's hair, curling, plaiting and weaving, using the tricks of her trade. It pleased her to be able to contribute. They had done so much for her. Accepted her in their circle without question – welcomed her with food and drink. And most of all, in her time of need – offered her sanctuary. How could she ever hope to repay them adequately?

Chapter 16

High on the mountain of the sun, above the Alhambra, in the gardens of the Generalife, Starla-sky awaited her turn to dance. The halls and courtyards rang with the deafening roar of the audience, in appreciation of the previous performers. How could she follow that? Quaking with first night nerves, superstition crowded her mind, striking a chord of inadequacy.

Amongst the most brilliant dancers, decked out in their lavish apparel, they came from far and wide - from all corners of Spain, Starla-sky felt like an impostor. They would laugh her off stage – expose her as a fraud. Such was the state of her thoughts as the violinists began and the compare announced with a sweep of his arm.

"Paco Herrera un Starla-sky Thorson…"

Starla-sky froze. Paco squeezed her hand and whispered encouragement. "Let's go for it. This is your chance to shine."

Heart pounding, she inhaled deeply and stepped out to centre stage. With Paco, strong and proud by her side, suddenly she was transformed. Adrenalin flowed, she felt alive – ten feet tall. Moving rhythmically into the dance she felt the audience emotions raise, animating pure energy. "Ole! Ole!" reverberated around her. This is me, this is my life, she thought, this is where I belong.

Together, Paco and Starla-sky made a striking couple, both blonde and beautiful. She looked sensational, like an exotic peacock in her blue and silver dress coordinating with Paco's electric blue outfit; a bewitching mix of colours and textures. Starla-sky's hair was arranged to one side, cascading over her shoulder, fastened with a white orchid.

She projected a whole range of emotions through her total submergence in the dance. The routine had been practised diligently and could not be faulted under the keenest scrutiny. Their steps harmonised perfection.

As they finally took their bow, the audience erupted into wild applause. An elated Starla-sky and Paco swept from the stage.

The music changed to dulcet tones and the compare announced. "Anita Velázquez!"

Slowly, Anita drifted across the stage with the sombre tune reflecting her mood of melancholy. Her eyes were large and sad, mirroring unrequited love. Gone was the sparkle. Her quiet gentle beauty was contradicted by the startling flame of her dress. She gave herself to the dance, conveying her agony into a gradual crescendo of passion; releasing resentment, healing through movement. The primitive tempo drew the audience until their hearts were pounding in time to the rhythm. A singer let out a harsh nasal howl. The song was one of oppression, lament and bitter romance.

Starla-sky watched from the wings, moved to stunned silence. Her emotions stirred by the portrayal of drama. She hated the very thought of loves destructive force. She wanted to rush on stage and end Anita's torment – tell her there was no need to grieve – that Paco returned her love.

The audience were ecstatic. After Starla-sky and Paco's vibrant demonstration, Anita's performance contrasted beautifully. Amid rapturous applause, Anita bolted like a young colt to lose herself in the serenity of the Summer Palace. Starla-sky grabbed Paco by the arm.

"Go to her," she urged. "Talk to her – I beg of you."

"Si – You are right. We have to straighten a few things out." He made his way through the throng to the entrance.

Starla-sky stayed to watch the sensual art of the flamenco. In this cultural setting there was none of the dishevelled display encountered at the gypsy caves. These were talented professionals honed to sophistication. There was no contorting like wild cats or pulling of hair in animal fury that at times she had witnessed. They showed their mastery of the dance with graceful controlled passion. She was caught up in the atmosphere of hand clapping to the buleria, fandango, jaleo and the virile farruca.

She began to wonder when José and Marcia would make their appearance. He had left the camp early to return the stallion. Presumably he had spent time with Antonio organising the festival events. She guessed their performance was to be the highlight of the evening.

By the time of the interval when Paco had not returned, she decided to take a wander through the water gardens. Passing a long pool surrounded by trees and tropical blooms, a row of water jets sprayed silvery over beds of roses and a variety of blossoms – scarlet and crimson, clashing pinks and bright blues.

In this idyllic setting Starla-sky fancied herself as Alice in Wonderland surrounded by cool greens, yellows and leafy ferns. She walked past scented banks and along the avenue of tall cypresses leading to the Alhambra.

In the fragrant cool silence she entered the court of myrtles, dominated by a still lake, framed by tall archways. Exploring the extraordinary charm of the place she came across a half hidden doorway which, according to the plaque, was once a king's residence. Unable to resist the temptation, and considering at this point it was deserted, she cautiously opened the door.

She gasped with admiration. Set out before her was an enclosed garden. An exquisite courtyard with arcades upheld by slender gold columns, carved in intricate designs. In the centre a fountain of crystal clear water was supported by twelve extravagant lions. This must be the Patio de los Leones, she recalled in amazement. Very odd – it felt familiar. Plaques of calligraphy on the walls seemed to be demanding her attention. Mesmerised by the mystical Egyptian Sanskrit, she failed to hear the approaching footsteps.

"They stand for the attainment of truth," said José, coming up behind her.

Starla-sky jumped in shock. "Oh! Where did you come from?"

"I've been looking for you. I saw Paco with Anita – and Paco informed me he had left you watching the performance. You should not be wandering around on your own."

"Don't fuss Jose. There is no one here," she replied. "Do you understand the writing on the wall?"

"Si – it is poetry and passages from the Koran. They carry the theme of paradise," he answered, and then gestured with a theatrical sweep of his hand. "This is the Court of Lions which conceals a complexity of subtle symbolism."

Starla-sky took in the elaborate Moorish architecture and raised an inquiring eyebrow. "Intriguing."

"If you recognise the inner meaning of the Islamic poetry, you will then observe the twelve lions represent the twelve signs of the zodiac," he explained. "The cardinal points flow out from the fountains – four channels – four corners of the cosmos."

"How interesting. There's something about this place – it's almost as if –" She closed her eyes to shut out her confusion, and then opened them and shook her head. "Tell me José, can you translate the words on these wall plaques?" It suddenly seemed very important.

"I could if I had all day. The interval will be over soon and it will be my turn to perform. Marcia will be waiting."

"Oh – of course," said Starla-sky, moving away to study the lions.

Jose glanced idly over the writings on the wall. "We must be getting back now. I will bring you another time and translate for you," he assured her, and then stopped in surprise. "Hey, this may interest you – look, its Paco's parents." A small plaque had caught his eye. It was obviously not as old as most of the others. He began reading slowly. "In celebration for my wife." He paused and looked at Starla-sky. "How romantic – it's a declaration of love," he remarked, before continuing, "Kirsten Herrera – on this day of our marriage." Underneath was written, Pablo Herrera.

Starla-sky, jolted out of her apathy, looked at Jose in shock. "What – what did you say – Kirsten – Herrera?"

"Why yes – she is Paco's Mother," he answered.

"But – it can't be José – that's my Mother's name."

José did not fully grasp what she was saying. He shrugged. "So – your Mother is called Kirsten too."

"Don't you think that's unusual? Kirsten in not a common name. And Paco said she was English. I never asked him what happened to his Mother. Did she die?"

"No – I think not," answered José. "His Mother went to England and never returned. Soon after, his Father died from an illness. He doesn't talk about it. His Grandmother, Rosario and the extended family brought him up. She lived at our camp then."

Starla-sky had gone white as a sheet. As it sunk in what he was saying, a conviction slowly dawned on her. It was too much of a coincidence. "I tell you - it is my Mother. Where can I obtain a copy of their marriage certificate?"

"You cannot. They had a gypsy wedding and gypsies keep no records."

"Well – who would have married them?" she asked.

"The holy man from the hills – he would have performed the ceremony. He has since deceased. But Rosario would have witnessed it. He passed the knowledge onto her."

"Don't you see what this means?" she stopped aghast with the realisation. "That makes Paco and I…"

José brushed a hand across his brow. Her implications were incredulous. He studied the wall plaque closely. "Your imagination is running away with you querido."

"No José – I think I've found my answer. Let's go and find Paco."

He laid a restraining hand on her shoulder. "I wouldn't advise springing your wild revelations on Paco in haste. He's buried the past – it goes deep with him. He cannot accept he was abandoned by his Mother. That is why he keeps her flamenco dresses, in case she returns someday."

"But I must tell him the truth." She gritted her teeth in desperation. "Surely someone knows Kirsten's maiden name?"

"Rosario – si, she will know."

Starla-sky jumped for joy. "What are we waiting for? She will confirm it – I know."

"Okay – I'll believe it when I hear it from Rosario's lips," relented José. He glanced at his watch. "We must hurry – I'm due to perform in ten minutes."

A display of fireworks lit the night sky above the Generalife gardens, adding to the excitement of the festival. José and Marcia's performance proved to be the climax of the evening. Throughout their dramatic routine Marcia scowled in fury. She was angry that José had returned from the interval with Starla-sky.

Deep in her own thoughts, Starla-sky was unaware of Marcia's hostility. She smiled at the sight of Paco and Anita standing close together. They only had eyes for each other. Paco laughed at something Anita said and Starla-sky saw him in a new light. It could not be her imagination…

The pace of the music increased. The twirling purples and magentas of Marcia's dress, flashed before Starla-sky in a kaleidoscope of brilliant colours. José's high waist black trousers and bolero, allowed Marcia complete attention. She had the assurance of one used to the dance. But still, she felt cheated. The audience, stimulated by her volatile vehemence, gave a standing ovation. Marcia pinned back her sleek black hair, which had fallen loose and flounced off.

Shouts of 'encore! encore!' filled the palace. It took José a good deal of coaxing to persuade her to return to the stage. As far as Marcia was concerned, no one could equal her. Before she would agree to a repeat performance, she demanded full recognition from the whole of her audience.

Starla-sky was now shaken out of her contemplation by the enthusiastic uproar. She stood with the crowd joining in the adulation. José and Marcia returned to dance. Starla-sky now paid full attention. She was impressed. They were indeed the stars of the show. She had to admit they made a perfect couple.

When the festival came to an end and the crowds departed, José disappeared with Marcia. Starla-sky returned to the caves with the gypsy dancers. The journey was accomplished with much laughter and singing, echoing through the darkness.

At the camp, the blackness of the night was illuminated by firelight. Paco and Anita were sitting around the fire with the gypsies. By their flirtatious behaviour, it was evident that their misunderstandings had been resolved. Starla-sky was loath to interrupt their intimacy. However, she had to speak to Paco. She found a space beside him and whispered in his ear.

"Will you come with me to see Rosario tomorrow? There is something we have to find out and it concerns both of us," she said.

Paco squeezed Anita's hand and grinned at Starla-sky. "That sounds secretive."

"I don't mean to alarm you, but I think it's important. Anita can come too."

"I take it you won't tell me what it's all about?" inquired Paco.

"It's best we see Rosario first. I think it's time she explained a few things to us," answered Starla-sky. "I'll leave you two alone now. See you in the morning. I expect I'll be asleep when you come in Anita – so good night."

"Good night Starla-sky." Anita leaned over to kiss her on the cheek. "And thank you," she whispered.

On entering the cave, Starla-sky lit the oil lamp by the shrine and knelt to offer a prayer of thankfulness before climbing into bed. She lay awake for a long time perusing over the incredible events of the day. A lot of questions, she hoped, were soon to be answered. Quietly, she spoke to the ancestors and asked that she might learn the truth from Rosario tomorrow. It pleased her that Paco and Anita were reconciled at last.

Her relief faded as her thoughts strayed to José. He and Marcia were made for each other and she had no doubt he was with her this very moment. After all, men wanted their offspring in their own image – her Aunt Eleanor had told her, had she not? It was an ego thing. Marcia with her similar looks to Jose could well provide him with this. Starla-sky with her Anglo Saxon appearance had no chance of competing. How many points, she wondered, was that to him? She had forgotten the game. It was foolish anyway – pointless, she realised now with an uncomfortable dull ache in her heart. Thank God Paco was not egotistical. Aunt Eleanor could always be wrong…

Early next morning Anita was not in bed when Starla-sky awakened. In the clear light of day Starla-sky began to worry. Somehow she felt responsible for the younger girl. She was sure Paco would not take advantage of the situation. But still, she felt protective towards Anita.

Hurriedly pulling on shorts and tee shirt, she went out to find her. To her surprise the women were already up and about, busying themselves, preparing food. Ana the cook was issuing orders to the young girls. Anita was adding herbs to an earthenware crock, filled with a strong salted liquid. She looked radiant, her old vivacity revived.

"What's going on?" asked Starla-sky.

"La bodo!" exclaimed Ana.

"La bodo? A wedding?" repeated Starla-sky in surprise. "Who's wedding?"

Ana just smiled and continued skinning a large marrow.

Starla-sky glanced at Anita to enlighten her, and then asked. "You did come in last night, didn't you?"

Anita giggled. "Of course I did. What were you thinking; I was out all night with Paco?" She looked aghast. "How could you question my integrity?"

"Sorry – I should have known better," smiled Starla-sky. "I'm glad you're happy though."

Anita grinned playfully. "So you should be. And yes – I am extremely happy."

"And this wouldn't have anything to do with a certain handsome young man we both know – would it by any chance?" probed Starla-sky teasingly.

"Ah! That's my secret," laughed Anita, tossing her head.

"I see," said Starla-sky, pleased that her friend was back to her carefree self again. "And where is the young man in question?" she inquired, eager to embark on their journey to Rosario.

Anita added the last chilli and head of garlic to the pot. She stirred the mixture. "We meet him in ten minutes. He hasn't forgotten – you have intrigued him - and me likewise."

Four men appeared, holding aloft, a whole suckling pig, reminding Starla-sky of the imminent wedding feast. If it was not Anita and Paco's wedding, whose was it? For some reason she did not want to know. With dread, she suspected it was to be José and Marcia. However, this morning she had more important issues on her mind.

Chapter 17

Starla-sky approached Rosario's wagon with her heart in her mouth. After all these years was she about to discover her heritage? Or would the visit prove to be fruitless?

Rosario was sitting in the doorway. "So – "she nodded gravely, "you have come – I have been waiting – you have discovered for yourself the truth?"

"I don't know," answered Starla-sky. "I have a question."

"I think you know the answer," hinted Rosario.

Perhaps Starla-sky did know the answer, but she wanted it confirmed. "Tell me Rosario – what was the full name of Pablo Herrera's bride?"

Paco shot an inquiring glance at Starla-sky. Anita stood still as a statue, while Rosario looked at each of them in turn. Starla-sky held her breath in the deathly silence that followed.

Eventually Rosario said slowly. "Kirsten Thorson. Si – I called her the angel – she came from out of nowhere."

Forgetting her usual reserve with the old woman, Starla-sky shrieked with glee and hugged the frail body. "It's true then. She was my Mother – and Pablo Herrera was my Father – and Paco –"she stopped, suddenly reticent.

Paco looked in a state of shock. Anita supported him with an arm around his waist.

"And not forgetting my Niña – me your abuela," reminded Rosario.

"Of course not Grandmother," Starla-sky said gently.

Paco stiffened. He was being forced to acknowledge his hidden childhood grief. "No! No!" he shouted. "She abandoned me - had a better life without me." He sat on the ground, put his head in his hands and blinked back bitter tears. He was that four year old boy again waiting for his Mother to return. Never had he admitted his feelings aloud before.

Starla-sky sank down on her knees before him. "No Paco – you are wrong. Most of my life I too believed she had abandoned me. She was killed in an accident. She was on her way to fetch you."

"Ah, so that is it," mused Rosario. "She was with child - si. There were problems with pregnancy – she had to return over the sea for help. Kirsten and Pablo communicate mind to mind. She would know he had left this world. I felt in my bones they were not parted."

Tears ran down Anita's cheeks, overwhelmed with emotion. She put her arms around Paco and Starla-sky. "I think it is wonderful," she managed between sobs.

A lump came to Starla-sky's throat. She could not speak.

Paco shook his head. "I can't take this all in. It's too much. God Starla-Sky, you certainly know how to spring surprises."

They looked at each other and began laughing and crying at the same time.

"Now – my familia," interrupted Rosario. "I think I revive you with a cup of el vino dulce, before you return to your lives." She went inside the wagon and returned with four cups of homemade brew. "We drink to truth and love that conquers all."

In unison they raised the red liquid to their lips. The wine relaxed them as they sat talking. Paco asked Starla-sky endless questions about the details she had heard about Kirsten, from Aunt Jessie. She in turn wanted to know all about their Father. Rosario listened with a knowing expression until it was nearing midday and time for them to return to camp.

"Starla-sky," whispered Rosario as they said their goodbyes and the other two had gone on ahead out of earshot. "You - come here this afternoon – on the hour of four. Don't forget now my Niña."

"Why?" inquired Starla-sky.

"Don't question. Just come," urged Rosario.

Starla-sky smiled gently. "Of course I will." She was intrigued. Perhaps Rosario needed to speak to her alone.

Paco thought it best to refrain from mentioning their kinship to the gypsies until everyone was gathered together in the evening. The whole camp was still in a state of preparation. After they had eaten a light lunch, Starla-sky felt obliged to take her place with the women at the brazier. Besides smoked hams and salted pork, she had never seen so much fish. Clams, razor shells, tuna, swordfish, anchovies, shrimps, langoustines and tiny delicious flatfish, which the women informed her were 'chanquetes' and 'angulas,' eaten piping hot in garlic sauce.

Not being much of a meat eater herself, Starla-sky looked forward to tasting the varied choice of fish. The wedding celebrations, she was not looking forward to. How would she feel when José and Marcia finally declare their love openly? Starla-sky was tense. Was it her imagination that everyone was acting strangely towards her? She was greatly relieved when it was time to slip away to see Rosario. If anyone could sort out her troubled feelings it would be her Grandmother.

Halfway up the hill to the wagon, Starla-sky could see a figure of a man advancing in the distance from the direction of the pine forest. Before she recognised him completely, she knew in her heart, it was José. She lost sight of him a couple of times behind small buildings and thickets. As she stopped in front of Rosario, sitting under the fig tree, he arrived from behind the wagon.

"Bueno – you both have come," stated Rosario.

Starla-sky glanced at José with apprehension. "What's this all about?" she asked.

José looked ahead stonily. "Relax," he murmured.

Rosario started to speak in some guttural dialect Starla-sky could not understand. She then produced two beautiful onyx stones on copper chains. "I have requested you both here Starla-sky to give you these onyx ancient witching stones." Slowly rising to her feet, she carefully stretched up and placed the mystical stone, first around José's neck, and then around Starla-sky's. "You wear at all times to be in tune with forces of nature. It protect you against evil that creeps up in the night."

Starla-sky's initial alarm subsided. She began to feel at ease. So this was the reason Rosario wanted to see her – to present her with this lucky charm. "Thank you for being so concerned about my safety. I am being well looked after," she smiled.

"That is good," replied Rosario. "Also – learn - meditate on stone. If you desire something strongly, direct your will towards it."

Starla-sky glanced again at José. He had not spoken a word. Tall and erect, his jaw set in determination. Standing close to him, for a moment, she experienced intense pleasure. She almost believed he was responsible for uniting her with her suppressed spirituality.

To her surprise, Rosario began chanting again in the peculiar dialect. It appeared she was concocting some sort of spell. This went on for some time, before falling silent. She then took José's hand and placed it ceremoniously on top of Starla-sky's; and in a low voice uttered a few more words. Then kissing them both on the cheek, she nodded at José as if to say, it is done. Starla-sky wondered what thoughts had passed between them.

Rosario looked exhausted. "Now – we take herbal tea."

Lifting the pot from the shade of some ferns, she poured it into cups and handed it to them. José passed his over to Starla-sky. Not knowing why, Starla-sky automatically passed hers to him. Eventually Rosario informed them she would have to go and lie down.

The intense chanting had obviously drained Rosario, thought Starla-sky as they left her and walked back down the hill. There was something extremely odd about the whole episode. She reached for the onyx stone and felt its smoothness in her palm.

"It was thoughtful of Rosario to give us this gift. I'll treasure it forever," she remarked, and then adopted a serious expression. "Gypsies have some strange customs, I must say. And what was all that chanting and joining of hands about?"

José hesitated for just a second, before looking her straight in the eye and declaring adamantly. "We are married."

Starla-sky caught her breath as if she could not believe what she was hearing. "You are joking!"

"No I am not Starla-sky." He stated calmly.

She choked in alarm. "We most certainly are not!"

He appeared to be amused by her outrage. "Think what you like querido," he said candidly. "I have a lot of work to attend to – so as my wife there will be certain expectations of you. This will keep you out of trouble and one less worry for me."

"What do you mean – expectations?"

"As a married woman you will not be permitted to visit the Taverna or stray from the camp. I warned you. You left me no choice. Seeing as you take too many risks I decided to bring our wedding forward."

"What wedding?" she replied indignantly. "I wasn't aware there was to be one – you haven't proposed! That is even if I wanted to marry you. You take too much for granted. And as for going to the Taverna - you can't stop me."

He was not to know she had already made her decision to keep away from the Taverna in future. Anita's distress had made her see the error of her wilful ways. She was not about to admit this to him now. It was typical of him to go ahead without consenting her. What arrogance!

"Why didn't you tell me what was happening?"

"Well. Would you have come?"

"I might have," she pouted. "No – I wouldn't."

"I think Rosario knows you better than you know yourself. She chose you for my bride. That is our custom," he informed her. "Our Grandmothers are the matchmakers. They hold our destiny in their hands. They are the wise women and see into our hearts."

Now she had discovered she was one of them, she tried to grasp what he was saying. Had her Mother also been chosen to marry Pablo by some divine intervention?

"It was just a matter of time. It was destined to happen sooner or later. I just brought it forward that's all." He shrugged as if his explanation was reasonable. "I was about to ask you that day at the Alhambra."

"Why would you want to marry me? I'm a flighty English girl remember?"

He ignored her retort. "It was not my wish for it to happen so soon. But after I found the dead eagle, I realised I had to keep you out of harms way."

"Hmm! It can hardly be a proper marriage." She passed a derisory glance over his casual clothes and her own creased shorts and tee shirt. "We hardly look like a bride and groom."

"Appearances are unimportant. I assure you we are married. Rosario inherited the right to perform the wedding ceremony from the holy man. He passed on his sacred knowledge when he left his body for the other world. We cannot escape our destiny. The reason will be made clear in time. We must put our trust in the Gods."

"You really believe that? Who would recognise such a marriage?"

"It has been ordained by Rosario. Gypsies have been joined together in this way for centuries. Your own Mother and Father took their blessing in the eyes of the ancestors. I understand from Rosario that you were right about your Mother being Pablo Herrera's wife. In my eyes you are no longer a flighty English girl, but one of us. And since I have discovered that you have no living parents to ask permission for your hand, I have been to see your Aunt and Federico. I discussed my wish to marry you with them and they gave their blessing."

"Really? I bet you never told them that I was not consulted!" She pressed her lips together stubbornly.

The sun was beginning to set above the mountains. Time had passed swiftly since they had set out to see Rosario.

"We had better get back for the celebrations," murmured Jose.

"Of course – the celebrations," she said wryly. And to think she had thought they were for José and… Marcia will be furious!

She scowled. "I don't feel like celebrating."

"We cannot disappoint the gypsies. They have been preparing for this wedding feast all day."

She sighed. It seemed there was no way out of this. She would have to play along with it, at least for this evening. José began to walk down the hill. He stopped to see if she was coming. She held her head high and followed him to the camp.

A crowd had gathered excitedly on the outskirts to welcome them.

"I seem to be the last to know," muttered Starla-sky under her breath.

José was smiling broadly.

It should be the happiest day of her life, she thought grimly. Anita ran to greet her. She whisked Starla-sky away from the boisterous gathering to the cave. Inside, a scarlet flamenco dress had been laid out ready on the bed. The tiered skirt fell from below the hips over layers of netting. The dress was lavishly embroidered; a circle of red roses for her hair and red satin shoes to complete the outfit.

"Gypsy brides wear the brightest dresses to celebrate their wedding," said Anita. "This was your Mother's wedding dress. You will shine like a brilliant star – like the love that shines in my brother's eyes for you."

Starla-sky looked suitably stunned. Was this really happening? Had they all gone mad? "Did you… You didn't…" She couldn't get her words out.

"Did I know? Yes I knew. It is written in our fate" Anita replied.

It was all happening so fast. It was as if Starla-sky was riding on a roller coaster, and through no fault of her own, found it impossible to jump off. Was it only this morning she had been convinced José would be marrying Marcia? This had not pleased her.

Now the unthinkable had happened. Is this what she wanted or not? There certainly was a spark between them – but marriage? She did not dare to admit that she could possibly be in love with him. They were so different. There was not a hope in hell it could work.

"How long have you known?" she asked.

"For some time I knew this – that José planned to marry you. But I thought you had other ideas. Then late last night he informed us all that he was going ahead. Do not be angry with him. It's for your own protection."

"I cannot believe you just said that. He doesn't love me."

"Rosario is never wrong," said Anita, and then continued with eyes sparkling. "Paco has asked me to marry him. Now I am of age. I will soon be twenty one. Most gypsy girls are married by the age of sixteen but Paco wanted me to be sure. He will be twenty seven the same month"

Lucky you to be asked thought Starla-sky. She sighed wearily. "Anita, I'm so pleased for you."

"You and I shall truly be sisters," laughed Anita excitedly. "Paco and I will wait for the next full moon for our wedding, to determine fertility."

Starla-sky lifted the dress half heartedly from the bed and stepped into it. Anita's praise fell upon dead ears. As if held prisoner in a living dream, Starla-sky gazed through the window in apprehension. She opened the door and walked out to experience, like all brides before her – the unknown.

Chapter 18

Beneath the luminous circular moon, José stood resplendent in silver. His waistcoat glittered – embroidered and studded with pearls. All around pulsated with vibrant voices, the sound of guitars and violins. In this spot, the praising of thousands of weddings had been witnessed before.

Starla-sky behaved as expected of her. She melted into José's arms for the first dance, amid cheers of encouragement. Young girls clapped, anticipating their own future weddings. Old women wept for long ago. The men drank to the lovers in envy of their youth. Long tables had been erected laden with an abundance of sumptuous food in honour of the newly weds.

The evening progressed to fever pitch, with volatile dancing and drinking; the darkness illuminated by the gaudy colours of the gypsies clothes, twirling in the moonlight. Starla-sky, caught up in the heady atmosphere, felt she was hurling headlong down a helter- skelter, while the music mounted and vibrated.

A short pause between dancing, when Paco called for a toast to the bride and groom and also announced the news that Starla-sky was his sister, only caused to heighten the elation.

By the time of the last dance, Starla-sky was lost in an alluring world of make believe. José held her close and breathed in her perfume. "My beautiful wife," he murmured. "How sweet is your fragrance? A bouquet of a thousand flowers in bloom."

"Wild rose," she replied breathlessly.

His cheek brushed sensually against hers. "It must be made especially for you querido. The aroma blossoms on contact with your skin."

His words made her feel incredibly tender towards him. She was dizzy with excitement.

"You cause me to dream about you," he continued huskily. "I long for you to keep me warm in winter."

She could feel the hardness of his body. The tension between them was making her feel light headed. In desperation she gasped. "You know a lifetime marriage is unrealistic."

The music stopped. He prized her arms from around his neck. Brushing her comment aside, he said. "I must go. Meet me in the pine forest when the moon goes down."

The shock of what he was suggesting sent a thrill piercing through her body. The sudden primitive urge to be possessed by him totally, body and soul, stole over her. She shivered.

"I will be waiting," he said seductively.

She knew instinctively that she would go. She could not help herself. As he left her aroused in the night, she caught the naked promise in his farewell glance.

Once the women realised José had departed, they fussed around her and told her they were to take her to the pool to bathe. They hurried along the path and peeled off her clothes by the shimmering water. She washed herself ritualistically with the rose gel, which Anita had fetched from the cave. There was no embarrassment on her behalf. It felt natural to anoint her body while the women looked on in admiration, teasing and commenting with good humoured advice on how to make a man happy in the night. It may have been considered raucous vulgarity in Starla-sky's former world. But here the married women reassured the new bride with tales on how to control the corrupt male with calculated surrender. He would then worship her forever.

Presently the women accompanied Starla-sky to the outskirts of the forest and with much chortling sent her in the right direction.

José was sitting silently in the gas light, directing his will on the onyx stone, towards the fulfilment of his desires. For the last few weeks, between his varied activities, he had secretly, been decorating a traditional wagon where he would bring his new bride – to make their home. Rosario had told him to pick sleeping rose apples from the trees at sunrise and lay them in the marriage bed. This, she assured would bring happiness and faithfulness. Rosario herself had been to the wagon today with a magic potion she had made out of the mossy growth on the twigs of the dog rose, and laid it under their pillows. José was in no doubt Starla-sky would come.

Through the thicket of trees, Starla-sky followed an overgrown path. Although the darkness hung like a thick blanket around her she was not afraid. She knew José was not far from the outskirts where the women lingered to guarantee her safety. Her breath was coming quickly now; her reasoning mind overpowered by a force beyond her control. It was no good; she had to be with this man. Finally she had to admit he filled her dreams – her every waking moment. At the sight of the wagon she started to run.

He arose as she entered. In a daze she heard her own voice. It was as if it was not her talking – as if the words were formed from another source – a side to her that had been waiting to surface – to set her free.

"José," she gasped. "Make love to me – now. I want to lay with you in the night – feel your skin pulsating against mine – the heat of your desire. I'm going crazy." A sob escaped from deep within her. Her passion was too much to bear. Never in her life had she felt such overwhelming desire.

He returned her wide eyed gaze. "Don't you think I want you too? It is tearing me apart."

She was ready for him, every inch of her aching for his touch. With trembling fingers she went to unbutton his shirt.

He controlled his thirst for her and caught her hands in restraint. "No – wait – not here." Effortlessly he lifted her into his arms and took her outside beneath the stars. "The first time will be special. We have to initiate the earth." Feverishly they clung to each other…

"Querido," he murmured huskily in a choked voice, "at last."

With hands shaking, she pushed him back. Tantalisingly she let her dress fall to the ground. Removing her lacy underwear she stood gloriously naked before him. He devoured her with his eyes, mesmerised – unable to move.

Boldly, she started to unbutton his shirt again. He moved one hand to the belt of his trousers. She caressed his body as she went, exploring the tautness of his muscles.

When he was as naked as her, he drew her to him, their skin smouldering with fire. This was the moment they had waited for. Together they fell to the ground.

"My sweet rambling rose," he whispered, as his lips found hers, and then moved down the curve of her neck and progressed to her ripened breasts, before continuing to every sensitive inch of her.

She moaned in submission. It was too much for him. In his urgency, he took her there and then. She had never experienced anything like it. Making love with the grass beneath their bodies; the scent of pine trees and fresh air caressing their naked skin -
intoxicating their senses. They were two passionate people. At that moment she was ready to sacrifice all her modern woman principles.

Late into the night, exhausted from their extraordinary day, they fell into bed and slept soundly, wrapped in each others arms.

Next morning Starla-sky awoke to find herself alone in the bed. She was disorientated for a moment. Where was she? Then it all came back to her. It was real. She was now married in the eyes of the gypsies. Oh my god, she thought. In the heady hypnotic atmosphere of the evening she had allowed José to possess her, mind, body and soul.

She got out of bed, slipped her dress on and opened the door. José was sitting on a boulder staring straight ahead. Cautiously she walked up behind him and put her arms around his shoulders and kissed him lightly on the cheek. He tensed and pushed her arms away.

"I need to be alone," he murmured.

She felt his rejection. "What is wrong José?" she asked. "Are you feeling ill?" She wondered if he had a hang over. But that would be unlikely for him.

"Starla-sky I need some space to think. I am going to walk in the mountains." He got up and turned away from her. "I will be back at noon and we shall eat." And with those parting words he was gone.

In bewilderment she sat down on the boulder. What had come over him? Did he now regret their union? She had been right – it could not work out between them. Now she had bonded with him, she wanted him more than ever. The situation had become intolerable.

The morning, she spent wandering around with her tortured thoughts. She managed to cook the ingredients he had left for a delicious soup. He returned at noon still in a distant mood. They ate their food together, neither of them attempting to speak. Presently, she could bear it no longer. Her need to be enveloped in his arms enticed her to reach out and touch him.

"Why are you so silent José? What have I done?"

He drew away from her, his thoughts conflicting in turmoil. The love, she had been so sure had shone in his eyes, when she came to him last night, had now hardened. There was something ugly that he had buried at the back of his mind. It surfaced now with his possessive nature and cut through him like a knife. Certain things he had not come to terms with – he could not bring himself to accept from his new wife. Sudden jealousy incited him to attack her verbally.

"That was a good performance last night! How convincing," he uttered brutally. "How many lovers did it take to teach you?" Her past illusory lovers, that she had so brazenly disclosed to him, now came back to haunt her. He could not forget.

Why did he have to spoil the beautiful moments of their wedding night? "It's not true José," she cried. "I lied. No one could compare to you."

"How can I ever believe what you say?" he stormed angrily. "If it wasn't for the fact that you are now my wife and a relative of Federico Ramon, I would sorely be tempted to leave you to the villains."

"How can you be so cruel? We have just shared the most intimate experience a man and woman can. You must believe me – I love you. Please say you believe me," she pleaded, not caring how she humiliated herself.

"You can stay here tonight," he stated coldly. "Don't bother to pack your clothes at the cave. Tomorrow you can return there, until the crime at the hotel has been solved. I will not hold you to our marriage arrangement. It is only binding in the eyes of the gypsies – so you are free to go," he said callously, and then added as it occurred to him. "I can't say I didn't enjoy last night and you cannot deny you found it pleasurable also. So, as you are still my wife whilst you remain at our camp, and if on occasion you need to satisfy your urges, you can come to me. I will be here to service."

Although she felt insulted, there was nothing she could say. She knew him by now. He was stubborn and no amount of cajoling would change his mind.

He was up on his feet, and turned away with indifference. "I have things to attend to. Do not wander too far this afternoon."

It was late when he returned. Starla-sky was sitting outside in the moonlight. The stony silence engulfed her. She felt trapped in a downward spiral. José went into the wagon and got into bed, rolled over and promptly fell asleep.

Lamely she followed him. Numb with consternation she dimmed the oil lamp and got into bed beside him. Despair took hold of her in the obscure darkness. Overdue tears finally spilled from her eyes. Like phases of the moon her moods had fluctuated rapidly the last two days, unsettling her equilibrium.

She had been ecstatic at the discovery of her lost parents – then apprehension at the news of a surprise wedding. That afternoon had incited her to disbelief and anger at José's plan for their marriage. Later, under false pretences she had believed herself deliriously happy with the arrangement.

He had lifted her to heaven when consummating their love. But he had tricked her. It was no more than a false promise. She had been deceived. So quickly it had turned to betrayal and ended in disaster. If only she had kept her self respect and resisted him. How foolish to have let herself fall into the trap of lustful desire. What was wrong with her to let this happen? For him it was mindless sex. All along, he no more thought they were truly married than she herself had wondered. He had used her heartlessly. With self loathing she buried her face in the pillow and sobbed silently with sheer exhaustion.

Their wedding night's short lived pleasure exploded in her mind like a thunder clap and disintegrated just as sharply. In the morning he was gone. She was not surprised. She glanced wearily over the interior of the wagon. He had obviously gone to a lot of trouble to furnish it; the decorations were exquisite. With a heavy heart she saw the note on a small brass table.

The words went straight to the point. To her disappointment there were no endearments or declarations of love. Her heart sank. She had half hoped for a miracle. But why should there be? She chided herself. He had made it only too plain where she stood with him. A convenient arrangement to satisfy their lust – that's what he had implied had he not? No more, no less. That's all she meant to him. She read the note again.

'I have business that warrants attention – will be gone all day. Go back to the camp. Adios. José' So impersonal, she thought. With mortifying resignation she dressed hurriedly. There was no way she wanted to stay a moment longer.

A dejected Starla-sky walked back to the camp - a forlorn figure. Drawing close she heard voices. She gritted her teeth and lifted her chin. On no account was she about to admit failure. Proud and straight she strolled through the chattering women to the cave entrance. A sudden hush descended around her. She glanced back towards them and gave them her most radiant smile.

"Buenos Dias," she said cordially. They returned her greeting in astonishment.

She opened the door, closed it behind her, leant against it and let out a long sigh.

"Starla-sky – what are you doing back so soon?" Anita sat bolt upright in bed.

"Oh!" Starla-sky jumped. She had not expected the younger girl to still be in bed. "Hi Anita – I - err - José has work to do, so I thought I'd come back – rather than stay alone."

"Work!" exclaimed Anita. "On your honeymoon?"

"Well yes, it's very important evidently and couldn't wait. Infact this unexpected urgent work will mean I will have to live here for awhile longer. Err – oh yes it's to do with my Aunt and Federico." Starla-sky said quickly, hoping this would explain her presence back at the camp.

This seemed to satisfy Anita, who then jumped out of bed and sympathised with Starla-sky's unfortunate predicament.

The days passed by serenely, undisturbed by the outside world. The two girls were able to rekindle their friendship and talked well into each night. Starla-sky spent most of her time at the school with Paco and Anita. Her Spanish was improving rapidly. She could take her place in the classroom and help teach the children. José had not once been to the camp and she wondered if he had indeed gone to Marbella. The gypsies true to form asked no questions.

Starla-sky's outward appearance was cheerful and calm. Inside, her mind was turbulent – a raging tornado waiting to happen. She had lost her appetite and couldn't sleep; tossing and turning all night. Since their wedding night José had become part of her and she could not dislodge him from her thoughts. Each night, his face swam before her and would not disappear when she closed her eyes. All her nerves were at breaking point with longing for him. Whether the marriage had been a sham or not, was irrelevant. They had bonded, and the spiritual and emotional involvement went too deep for her ever to be the same again.

The pull was too great. She held out for as long as she could, before being drawn like a magnet to the woods. He just had to be there! Leaving the gypsies dancing late one evening, she slipped away and ran towards the pine forest. Through the fields, past the streams into the thicket of trees - snagging her dress on thorns as she went. Her arms were scratched; she did not care. All that mattered was that she was with him again. She craved his touch.

His name escaped her lips in a gasp as she entered the wagon. "José – José," she breathed.

He let the onyx stone fall from his grasp. She caught the glint of flame in his eyes as he feverishly ripped at the buttons on her dress. "You have come querido?" His lips curved laconically – mocking her.

"Yes - yes," she managed unashamedly.

Her clothes scattered carelessly on the floor around them, roughly he dug his fingers into her flesh, pausing at her breasts, kneading, biting –

licking. She cried out in ecstasy. Impatiently she tugged at his shirt. It was unfair of him to remain fully clothed and not let her enjoy his naked skin. The rough material chaffed her body.

He prized her away and kissed the glowing pink of her stomach, which had been pressed hard against him. Between her moans of delight, she took the opportunity to unzip his trousers. The sight of his unleashed manhood sent her into a frenzy of excitement. Aroused to the point of no return, their eyes met in wanton unspoken agreement. His urgency matched hers. With savage abandon he flung her onto the bed and threw himself across her. With joy she received the full force of him deep into her being.

This emotional act seemed to unite them temporarily. Afterwards they lay kissing and fondling like any other newly weds. Their forced parting had incited an insatiable appetite for one another. José looked upon sex as an art form. Each time was different from the last. He really cared how she felt all the time, taking his pleasure from hers. Alone in the wagon, well secluded from society, they lost all inhibitions. The harmonious meeting of their bodies expanded her consciousness. He took her to multiple orgasms before reaching his own.

At dawn, José sat on a cushioned stool and poured them each a glass of wine. Starla-sky sipped the liquid slowly, and then placing the glass on the brass table, climbed astride him. Gently, he stroked the contours of her body and buried his head in her hair. She wound her legs around his back, brushing the tips of her breasts against the hardness of his chest and moved in tune with the rhythm of the night.

Chapter 19

In the morning Starla-sky returned to the caves. José had been absent from the marriage bed again, when she awakened. Not once had he apologised to her for his behaviour on their wedding night. It was as if he had blanked it out. But she knew it was not forgotten. Although he had enjoyed there love making, nothing had really changed.

She vowed she would never go back again to be treated as his plaything. She managed to last out for a week at a time before weakening and breaking her vow. The more she went to him, the more difficult it became to keep away. Each time he penetrated her body, illuminated her whole being. She lay with him on warm evenings outside with the stars above them in the sky.

He initiated her into the secret ancient Tantric practises passed down the generations; brought with the ancestors from the plains of India. They sat opposite gazing into each others eyes in meditation; at times she experienced the divine. Her energies raised, he took her to such profound places in their love making she had never dreamed of.

He was like a drug; she was hopelessly addicted. She began to have withdrawal symptoms if she was away from him for too long. She was losing weight and suffering palpitations. What had become of her? Why had she allowed herself to be possessed?

Thoughts of him had taken over her life. He was gradually winning the game hands down. Each time he took her to heaven. The way he looked at her, his touch was a pure physical thrill. She despised the weakness of her flesh.

One morning, she awakened with the yearning for José, knawing away at her insides, and decided her life had got completely out of control. She might as well be dead than be a slave to love. She was in grave danger of sliding away from reality and realised with terrible accuracy that she was in a similar position to her former relationship with Matt. Only now it was worse with the added complication of a mock marriage. She had lost herself. After all she had pledged to eradicate her past mistakes. It could not continue.

In desperation she went to the one person she knew held the answer.

"You are sad my Niña," said Rosario sympathetically, taking in Starla-sky's desolate expression. "Every time a woman is sad it is because of a man. So - it is Jose – si?"

"Si Rosario," murmured Starla-sky.

"Oh my chica – you have to learn men are not your enemy."

Starla-sky's crestfallen face looked at her beseechingly. "I have tried. Men are so complicated."

"No – they are different – that is so. That is what makes the attraction."

"I don't want to be attracted. I hate this feeling! It causes me nothing but pain."

Rosario let out a throaty laugh. "You are not the only one and you won't be the last."

"I love him, but it's destroying me." Starla-sky brushed away a tear.

"There can be no denying these differences between man and woman lead to confusion," said Rosario. "You must meet on middle ground."

"There can only be meeting of our bodies, not meeting of our minds. Our differences go way beyond the boundaries of mere man and woman." Starla-sky blushed at her confession.

"Niña," Rosario looked at her steadily. "Whether you are aware of it or not, you knew before your birth into this life, what your destiny would be. And the trials you would have to endure. That is why there is such a strong attraction between you and José." She took hold of Starla-sky's hand. "You have lived many lives with José and are now drawn together once more for the outworking of deep karmic lessons for your souls."

Starla-sky shook her head. "What am I to do? I've provoked him beyond endurance. I was so stupid to lie to him."

"There is no easy answer. It is written in your stars. You will endure emotional pain. You, more than others need a soul to soul union. First you must learn to love yourself. It is the most potent love of all. Dismiss the desires of earthly mind – trust in awareness of your higher spiritual self. Then you will find love return."

"But how?"

"Discipline your thoughts. We are but what we think. Follow the conscience of your heart. Do not let your body and mind do as they please. Control them. This is the secret. There is no other way. This is the narrow path – think on it."

"I understand," answered Starla-sky. If only José would try to understand her. Try to meet her halfway to reconcile their differences. Rosario spoke wisely. She gave her strength.

A note was waiting for Starla-sky when she returned to the cave. José had been and gone. A lump came to her throat. She ripped open the envelope. He wrote he was going away and would return at the waning moon. She screwed the paper into a ball and sat down with resignation. Maybe it was a blessing.

The next few months, besides allowing her space, also gave her the chance to prove herself with hard work and devotion to the school children. Teaching fulfilled her mentally. Emotionally her heart was breaking. She found it difficult to eat and sleep. Her drained appearance was beginning to be of concern to her companions. Rosario had said it wouldn't be easy.

Paco and Anita had been so busy; they had postponed their wedding until a future date. It would be delayed at least until José's return.

Winter had set in before any more news of José reached them. Paco returned one evening from the taverna in the Village de Carlos with a telegram addressed to him. It was just a short note to say that he was fine and to pass on to Starla-sky that things were going well…

The Sierra Nevada mountain area proved to be bitterly cold in November. Although an existence removed from the mainstream of life was fine, in Starla-sky's circumstances it was a distinct disadvantage. She began to miss the convenience of the telephone. Without one there was no way of contacting the outside world.

It was possible there had been developments in Marbella concerning the villains and José was giving her Aunt and Federico his support. There were times she was sorely tempted to take the journey back there herself to find out. Thoughts of ruining their strategic plans and causing worry to a great many people who had her best interests at heart, stopped her doing anything foolish.

Her present dilemma was not made any the easier by the change in temperature. The hot summer had been gratifying. To be able to live a harmonious outdoor life was at the chore of gypsy existence. In the not too distance past they would have left the caves in winter and made their way in convoy across the plains to a warmer region, away from the mountains. The social revolution had ended the nomadic life. It was replaced with an inbred hostility born of distrust and a fierce defence of their own territory.

Starla-sky now had an affinity with them, through her parentage. That her Father had been a well respected man of their community uplifted her self esteem considerably. If she had lived the majority of her life far from Spain, it was immaterial and obliterated completely from the minds of those around her. She was, she realised, part of them. She could be wild – corrupt even. Had she inherited these unsavoury traits, she wondered. Was this why she found it hard to control her powerful raging desires?

Each night she held the onyx stone and prayed fervently. Sometimes she would stand before the shrine and ask the ancestors to rescue her from her own destructive nature. Her longing for José ate away at her soul. Such was her torment. In her lowest moments, she cried out for mercy to take away her emotional pain. To sleep was her only peace.

Gradually a slow shifting in her consciousness began to take place. A gentle calm emanated from her. It was not that she had merely resigned herself to her fate; for she was not to know what that would be. Infact, she had become unsure of her future role. The one thing she was sure of was her spirit had been buried in darkness.

With time, her spirit awakened and grew strong like the blossoming of a seed into flower. Soon her appetite, which had been spasmodic, returned. On reflection, she was no longer the naïve English rose that boarded the plane in June, intent on adventure. If it was, as Rosario had explained, experiences good and bad that would mould one's character, today she was indeed the richer.

A sudden inclination had brought Starla-sky to the wagon in the woods. At times she had imagined it was this place that had bewitched her and maybe she could banish a few ghosts. But no – she could not pass the responsibility onto a place. There were no demons here.

In the small clearing amongst the trees, the caravan presented a peaceful haven of tranquillity; it welcomed her. Sunlight pierced through the branches, bouncing off the windows, dancing its pattern in the cold breeze. She was glad of the thick shawl that Anita had lent her.

It was her intention to tidy the interior, but she found the door locked. If she had not been so impulsive and decided to come on the spur of the moment, she would have realised it was no surprise. Whatever else José was, he was not stupid. He was bound to keep the wagon locked. She sat down on the step to rest.

Half an hour had passed in gratifying solitude, when she heard the sound of an approaching vehicle through the snow. Long shadows crept across the rising sun in the pines.

José eased the jeep to a halt on the woodland track. Starla-sky watched him walk towards her. He looked different – more subdued. The sharpness of his black eyes seemed softer, light played in their depths. His hair had grown a little too long, forming curls. The distinctive gold band glinted from his ear against the tautness of his olive skin. She had enough self control now not to fling herself into his arms. It had been a long time.

"Starla-sky," he said gently. "Anita told me you were here."

"Yes I'm here," she answered flatly. It sounded like a statement. Why had she said that? It was obvious she was here.

"Si – let us go inside." He leant across and put the key in the door. "It's cold out here."

He looked frozen despite the long thick black serge coat. She stood up and moved aside. Then in silence she followed him in.

"I have news for you," he said casually.

She lifted her eyes expectantly.

"You were right," he informed her. "It was your Johnny Spears. I have been tailing him for some time. He was spotted by my men in that building opposite the hotel. He used it to store stolen property – he was a small fish. We traced the brains of the operation who threatened Federico. He knew we were closing in and laid low for awhile. But due to Johnny Spears carelessness, they were flushed out. The police arrested him for theft.

"That's good news," she said, and then added. "I guess that means I can go back to Marbella."

"I suppose so," he murmured.

"Did you find out who the mysterious horse rider was?" she asked hastily.

"Si – that was Johnny Spears also," he grimaced. "And there's something else – Marcia – she told him where you were."

"Oh!" exclaimed Starla-sky. "But why?"

"Jealousy – I guess. You posed a threat to her," he replied.

Starla-sky declined to ask why. His answer might prove too intimate for her to cope with at present. She guessed the reason.

Silence hung heavily between them. It dawned on Starla-sky that a change had come over him. He was merely informing her of the facts and had reverted to the bodyguard relationship.

"Your Aunt is a very interesting lady," he suddenly commented. "Si – I had many talks with her."

"Oh – that's good," she answered blandly and turned her face to the window.

He continued. "She has given me an insight into certain circumstances."

She glanced back at him enquiringly.

"How a persons views in life are shaped…" he explained, adding, "you for instance."

"Me?" she wondered what was coming next.

He looked down at the floor and said softly. "Sometimes – one makes hasty judgements."

"Really?" she replied indifferently.

Another tense silence followed. José stiffened. He was becoming exasperated.

"Hell Starla-sky!" he banged his fist on the table, making her jump. "Madre de Dios – will you communicate with me? You are not making this any the easier. What I'm trying to say is…" He took a deep breath. "I'm sorry." It wasn't easy for him to apologise.

She stared at him. They both went to speak at once.

"After you…" she said.

"I learnt a lot while I was away. I've been an idiot." He looked at her intently. "Don't you know I have never been in love before until I met you – you've taught me the meaning of the word? I had this preconceived idea of how a relationship should be. I was wrong." With this admission he had laid himself bare.

"Oh – José…" Tears sprang to her eyes.

"Don't – don't. Just hear me out. Through your Aunt, I have come to understand where you are coming from," he took her hand. "I have no wish to take you away from civilisation – deprive you of the life you've always known. I make my money from horse breeding and flamenco – and use it to finance the school to educate the children. But if you wish to live in Marbella – I can afford to buy a villa there. That is – if you want to be my wife?" He stopped, his face softened. "Starla-sky – will you be my wife?"

She fluttered her eyelashes. "I – I thought you were angry," she stammered.

"Not any more. Your Aunt made me see that you can sometimes be very mischievous. I guess it's a common trait that runs in the family – laughing in the face of convention."

"I've never been promiscuous José," she whispered.

"I know querido. I was jealous. I was blind. We must learn to let go of the past. Learn to forgive – and meet each other halfway. We can learn from each other – I'm willing. The best thing about arguing is making up – eh?" He smiled gently.

She was tired of fighting. Suddenly she didn't want to play the game any more.

"Well – do you want this marriage to continue?" he asked. "Or do you still think a lifetime of marriage is unrealistic?

She looked at him and her heart missed a beat. "I've grown up José. I want full commitment."

"In that case I think it only fair to you, if we have our union blessed in the church of Santa Ana, in Granada."

"I would like that – but it's not necessary."

"I think it is," he insisted. "And – your Aunt and Federico shall be present."

"I do believe you've all been conspiring behind my back." She put her hands on her hip in mock annoyance.

"Well – your Aunt did say we could use the villa for our honeymoon," he confessed.

"You conniving…" She went to hit out at him playfully, aiming for his shoulder.

He caught hold of her hand and pulled her towards him. "I want to be part of your world, as you are of mine," he said in a low voice. "I was told of your dedication at the school – your selfless hard work. Although at first the women thought your ways alien – you now have acquired vecinded."

"Belonging!" she acknowledged.

"Si – the gypsies have accepted you. You have the right of belonging."

She nodded agreement. "I feel a rapport with them. I've come to know them well these past months and sympathise with their way of life. Teaching the children has given me satisfaction." With hindsight they had been the saving of her sanity.

He kissed her softly on the cheek. "I've missed you," he whispered.

She could hardly believe it – all her dreams were coming true. It was not that she had changed him, for she knew she could never do that. All she had ever wanted was his respect and in giving her this, he had brought about a change in himself.

"And I you, more than you'll ever know," she answered.

"But I'm glad I went away. It was a blessing in disguise. It gave me time to think and come to my senses. Distance gave me a better perspective," he explained, and then added. "You see – I didn't want to frighten you, but – I didn't find the eagle owl in the hills. It was dumped outside my door with a note that if I didn't leave well alone, the next bullet would be for you." His jaw tightened. "With a little help from me and my men, those vermin won't be bothering Federico and your Aunt again."

"I'm sorry I wound you up like that. I shouldn't have lied. I have been so foolish? You've done so much for me and my family." She searched his face for reassurance. "How can I ever thank you?"

"I'm sure I can think of something," he answered. A slow smile curved his lips as he gathered her into his arms.

Chapter 20

Starla-sky awoke the next morning with a smile on her face. She had stayed the night with José in the wagon and had never felt happier. José was already up making coffee. She lay sleepily thinking of all the amazing events that had led up to this moment. Since she had arrived in Spain so much had happened. It had been overwhelming. She had learned so much. Although she'd had to go through all the drama, she now listened to José softly singing as he made their breakfast and thought herself the luckiest girl in the world.

The tinkling sound of goat bells on the mountainside made her aware of how far away from England she was. A pang of nostalgia hit her. It wasn't that she wanted to go back to that life. She knew exactly where she wanted to be, but suddenly she had the urge to speak to her best friend Laura. She knew Laura would be wondering how she was. There was so much to tell her.

José came in with the tray. "Are you awake querido? Here's your breakfast."

She stretched her arms and sat up against the pillows. "Thank you – you are spoiling me," she said a little coyly.

He got in beside her and put his arm around her. "You deserve it my love. I look forward to spoiling you forever more." He kissed her on the forehead.

"Jose?" she said after they had eaten.

"Yes querido?"

She snuggled up to him. "Do you think we could find a telephone? I would really love to speak to my friend Laura in London. We haven't had any contact since I've been here with all that's been going on. And I feel the need to speak to my best friend."

"Of course you must," he said immediately. "We can go to the Village de Carlos. There's a telephone at the Inn."

Starla-sky dialled Laura's number at Raymonde's hoping she would be free to talk.

Laura answered the phone. "Oh my God - Starla! How are you? It's wonderful to hear your voice. I've been thinking of you."

"Oh Laura – I don't know where to begin. So much has happened. I've found my family. I have a brother and grandmother. And guess what I'm married – or I'm getting married," she gabbled excitedly.

"What! What do you mean – you are married or you're getting married?" Laura shrieked.

"I don't know what I mean. You see I am married in some respects – but we are having another wedding. Laura he's the most wonderful man. I can't tell you…"

"That's fantastic news. I'm so happy for you," enthused Laura. "But I don't understand. How can you be married in some respects?"

"It's a long story. You wouldn't believe it if I told you. I really hope you and Giovanni can come and visit us. I would love you to be at our wedding. I know its short notice."

"Oh yes! You can't keep us away. We'll come for a holiday. Oh God this is so exciting."

"That's great. I will tell you everything when I see you. And Laura how is everything with you?"

"I'm fine. You know how it is – still working for Raymonde. Giovanna keeps me happy. And – oh – Starla, I have some news about Matt."

"You know he phoned me here once. I put closure to it," replied Starla-sky.

"Yes – I gather so," said Laura. "He's been pestering me for news. Evidently he's been desperate to get hold of you ever since. Did you know he's been phoning your Aunts hotel continuously? I don't know what you said to him but his ego has obviously been hurt. Just goes to show you doesn't it? When you back off and he can't have you he comes running."

"Funny how human nature works isn't it? I told Aunt Jessie to ignore any calls from him."

"The thing is," went on Laura. "He's now gone off with that weird sect he belonged to and I heard he contracted a sexual disease. Oh yes – and Giselle Russell was in such a state, she's now having counselling."

"Oh my God! I almost feel sorry for her. Infact I do."

"You had a lucky escape Starla!"

Standing beside Paco, José fidgeted with nervous impatience. He turned his head to the rear, as the door creaked open. Shafts of winter sunshine streamed through the little church of Santa Ana. His eyes lit with love at the sight of Starla-sky, delicately supported on Uncle Lawrence's arm. An entourage of gypsy children followed – supervised by Anita; all dressed in a froth of matching violet.

She caught sight of Laura and Giovanni smiling fondly at her and thought her life just couldn't get any better.

José had never seen Starla-sky look lovelier – a vision in ivory shantung, her glorious hair adorned with white roses. It was all too much – he was overwhelmed.

"You are so beautiful querido," he gasped. "I love you so much. You make me the happiest man in the world." He was oblivious to anyone but Starla-sky.

Colour rose to her cheeks with pure happiness. She looked radiant. It was obvious to everyone there that they were crazy about each other. He could not keep his eyes off her.

Uncle Lawrence, who had been only too pleased to be asked, proudly escorted her to the altar, and then took his place beside his wife. Aunt Eleanor had decided to put up with the heat for a few days, and besides she wanted to see for herself how affluent her sister had become. She sat stiffly beside Federico and a beaming Aunt Jessie. Starla-sky smiled adoringly at José; her eyes appreciating his handsome appearance. His midnight blue suit was complimented by a white shirt with a frill from collar to waist.

They had wanted a quiet affair, but once the news circulated, no gypsy at the camp could be kept away. The church was filled with rejoicing. Outside an overflow of people waited to greet the newly weds – or newly blessed as Starla-sky had pointed out to José.

"Truly blessed," he had answered.

Sacred doves frozen on stained glass windows overlooked their solemn vows. Uncle Lawrence produced a thick gold band and José placed it on her finger. He bent his head and kissed her.

Aunt Jessie dabbed at her eyes with a handkerchief. Outside, the gypsies formed an arch for José and Starla-sky to walk through and began singing to send them on their way.

Starla-sky discarded the embroidered shawl on the bed and sat down in the chair. It had been a perfect day. The sun had continued to shine throughout the entire wedding ceremony. Aunt Jessie and Federico had decided to take a long holiday in Ibiza to recuperate from their ordeal of the last few months. They insisted Starla-sky and José stay at the villa in Puerto Banus. Uncle Lawrence and Aunt Eleanor were staying at the hotel for a couple of days before returning home. Laura and Giovanni had hired a villa and Starla-sky was looking forward to spend time with them before their flight home.

José put down the cases on the bedroom floor and removed his jacket. Starla-sky wandered over to the window and looked across at the blue ocean beyond. Her thoughts strayed to that London street a lifetime ago.

"And just to think," she murmured. "That old Tinker woman was right after all. There were times she had suspected it was José and not Johnny Spears she associated with the old crones warning – 'beware of the initial J.'

José came up behind her and squeezed her around the waist. "Sorry querido – what did you say?"

She turned to face him, her eyes alive with love. "Nothing darling - I was just thinking how incredible twists of fate are – and how lucky I am."

"I'm the lucky one," he said nuzzling her ear.

"When did it hit you?" she asked. "When did you realise you loved me?"

"It was instant attraction," he said, lifting her up into his arms. "Come to me my devil woman."

She laughed throatily and wound her slender legs temptingly around his waist. "I don't believe you."

"I fell in lust with you – the first time I saw you."

She punched him playfully. "So – it wasn't a love that grows slowly then?" she taunted.

"No – a special chemistry existed – connecting us." He spun her around laughing.

She was floating on air. "I confess I felt in too – I didn't want to admit it. It upset my plans."

He held her tight and swung her to the side. "I know – I was cruel. I tested you to the limit."

"Hey stop," she protested. "I'm going dizzy."

"You'll survive," he teased, and then said. "Our love survived against all the odds." He set her down, put some music on and whisked her into a slow dance. "I would like you to partner me next year at the festival."

She raised an inquiring eyebrow. "Marcia won't be thrilled."

"Marcia is history. We won't be seeing her again. She has married a rich Count – Alphonso Tenorio and has gone to live in luxury in Seville."

"You know – I thought you and she – "began Starla-sky.

José threw his head back and laughed. "Where on earth did you get that idea? You with your wild imaginings," he grinned devilishly.

"What's so funny?" she asked.

"I'm not mocking you. I was just thinking of when we first met – remember?"

"Hmm! How can I forget?"

"The first time I saw you I was enraptured. Your skin smelt of roses." He pulled her closer. "Ever since then I've had this recurring dream about you in the shower."

She smiled wickedly. "Well - what are we waiting for?" She began unbuttoning the back of her dress.

He watched in wonder as the gossamer shantung silk fell to the floor. To his delight she enticingly removed her white satin underwear. Moving lightly past him, she stepped into the shower room, inviting him to join her.

He hurriedly removed his clothes. Lifting the scented gel from the ledge, he began at her shoulders, moving sensually to her creamy contours and swells, lathering, caressing. He moulded her supple body like a sculptor, pliable beneath his sensitive hands.

"I swear you've lost weight – you're so slim querido," he said with a worried expression.

She trembled. "Love is my food." He was not to know she had been pining for him.

"Don't lose these – will you," he teased, squeezing her breasts.

She took the gel from him and covered him slowly from head to feet. With a flush of pleasure, she was aware of the arousing affect it was having on him. Every nerve ending of his body was sensitized; the perfume of roses enchanting their senses. Amongst the intoxicating bubbles of wild aroma, she yielded to him. Sweet jerks of sensation overtook her in ecstasy.

Afterwards as she lay in the bed within his arms, she whispered. "The wall has finally been dismantled."

"Um?" he murmured sleepily.

"It was something Rosario said to me." She leant up on her elbow and slid an arm across him possessively. "José – take me back to the wagon and hold me captive for as long as you wish."

"I will never hold you captive querido," he whispered. "You are free spirit. If you come – you come by your own admission."

"Willingly," she smiled. "And – will you teach me to horse ride?"

"Of course. It is only fitting that the wife of José Velázquez must be an adept horse woman. We shall be equal partners." He held her close, his eyelids heavy.

"Good night my husband – my very soul," she breathed softly against his chest.

Whether it was Rosario's love potion or just inescapable fate, Starla-sky would never know. They were together and that was all that mattered. Whatever the future would bring, they were there to support each other in all the joys and through the trials and tribulations of life. She knew there was untapped power out there that man had forgotten – perhaps through his own misuse. For the secrets of the universe must be harnessed for good and guarded closely from those whose only desire is evil and their own selfish gains.

The new moon shimmered through the blinds, gently touching the sleeping couple with its light. Starla-sky sighed contentedly in her dreams, encircled in the safety of José's arms.

Printed in Great Britain
by Amazon